THE PRIVATE DIARIES OF THE
EMPRESS MARIE-LOUISE

MARIE LOUISE

Frontispiece.]

THE
PRIVATE DIARIES OF THE
EMPRESS MARIE-LOUISE
WIFE OF NAPOLEON I

WITH INTRODUCTION AND COMMENTARY BY
FRÉDÉRIC MASSON
ACADÉMIE FRANÇAISE

WITH PORTRAITS

WILDSIDE PRESS

CONTENTS

LIST OF ILLUSTRATIONS

[*Photos by permission of Paul Laib, West Brompton, S.W.*]

THE
PRIVATE DIARIES OF THE EMPRESS MARIE-LOUISE

CHAPTER I

INTRODUCTION

IN 1918 I received a communication from London in which Lady Thompson invited me to consider a Diary of the Journeys of the Empress Marie-Louise, which had been bequeathed to her, with a view to its publication. I accepted this proposal with much pleasure, and shortly after received the manuscript, the contents of which convinced me of its authenticity.

This manuscript, the size of note-paper, is bound into a red morocco volume, the covers and fly-leaves being lined with green satin. The script is contemporaneous with the early years of last century, being regular and well-formed. At first it did not appear to me to be the handwriting of the Empress; the perusal of the text, however, removed all doubt as to its origin.

In answer to my inquiries as to how this manuscript had come into her possession, Lady Thompson forwarded me a letter from her grandmother, Mrs. Smijth Windham, which runs as follows:—

7

"In the year 1836 I became acquainted with a Swiss governess, called Mdlle. Müller, who lived many years with Lady Jane Peel. She was very intimate with a governess I had for my children, and I came into the room one day as she was reading these Memoirs to her friend. I stopped to listen, and then borrowed the book, which amused us much.

"Some months after this I proposed to her to let me purchase it, and after some hesitation she agreed.

"All she knew of it was, her brother Monsieur Müller was tutor to one of Marie-Louise's pages who was in waiting when she escaped from the Tuileries ; he picked it up from the floor and gave it to his tutor some time afterwards.

"The page's name is written in small characters on the first leaf of the book—Vicomte de * . . .—I forget the name. This is all I know.

"Kath. Smijth Windham."

Nevertheless, there are cogent proofs to demonstrate the authenticity of the manuscript. It is divided into three parts ; the first records the Imperial journey in the departments of Northern France and Belgium, between April 27 and May 13, 1810 ; the second comprises the journey of Marie-Louise to Mayence from July 23 to August 9, 1813 ; the third, her journey to Cherbourg from August 23 to September 5, 1813. These three journeys mark important epochs in the Emperor's history ; the first was made in the full enjoyment and splendour of a destiny

---

* The name of the page is pencilled so faintly that it is now illegible. —H. K. Thompson.

fulfilled ; the second and the third were undertaken when sinister rumours were in the air, when treason was breeding, when the very basis of the system, the Austrian Alliance, had been destroyed.

It appeared to me indispensable to place these three episodes in a setting that would bring out their full value and significance. While it would be impossible to describe the other journeys made by Marie-Louise in detail, it seemed advisable not to ignore them altogether.

The first, which began at Braunau, March 16, 1810, and ended at Compiègne on the 27th, was followed by many others apart from what were termed the *petits voyages* or excursions, which involved a life of insufferable nomadism, devoid of any permanent centre.

The Diary commences on April 27, 1810, the journey during which Marie-Louise jotted down the first pages. This was followed by a period of delicate health and the birth of the King of Rome. From May 27 to June 4, 1811, she travelled in Normandy, and no diary of that journey has hitherto been discovered. Between September 19 and October 11, she made a journey to Belgium, Holland, and the Rhenish Provinces, where for several days her correspondence with the Emperor formed a diary. In 1812, Napoleon left Saint-Cloud on May 9 with Marie-Louise, from whom he parted at Dresden on the 29th. She went from there to Prague, where she remained until July 1, going thence on the 7th to Würzburg, where she stayed for a week. On the 18th she arrived at Saint-Cloud. On December 18 the Emperor returned to Paris.

Next we have the two journeys recorded below : those of 1813 to Mayence, where the Empress joined her husband, and the one to Cherbourg, where she attended the opening of the dock.

During 1814 there was the terrible journey to Blois, which signified abdication ; likewise the journey of the disillusioned Empress to Vienna, and then the journey to Aix, and that *Excursion aux Glaciers de la Savoie* as recorded by the pen of Méneval, or perhaps by that of Neipperg, if he committed himself to paper.

Such was the Imperial life and destiny of the Arch-Duchess. We shall part from her at the journey to Blois, but we may link up the vicissitudes of her career as Empress by means of well-established facts and other documents indited by Marie-Louise herself. To this end I have made frequent use of a book which I published some years ago,* with the addition of certain letters by which we are permitted to penetrate the intimate thoughts of Marie-Louise, to appreciate her sentiments, to judge her ideas, and to determine whether we shall perpetuate the curse with which the French nation has branded her ; or whether, following the example of Napoleon himself, we shall look upon her with a certain indulgence as a weak vessel, fettered by obedience to tradition, carried away by temperament, and enslaved by mediocre ambitions.

FRÉDÉRIC MASSON.

Paris, *November*, 1920.

* *L'Impératrice Marie-Louise* (1809–1815) : Frédéric Masson.

CHAPTER II

THE House of Austria, which had dominated the world and held up the course of the sun in its States, was in 1809 reduced to lamentable indigence. Deprived of its army, revenues, and most of its possessions, some happy chance alone could reinstate this Empire in its former position. Austria was apparently at the point of death, and the oligarchs who ruled her and used her as a mask, were concerned lest she should expire.

The House of Hapsburg-Lorraine is one of the most remarkable in Europe, and claims a brief consideration.

After having occupied the Imperial Throne for three centuries, the House of Hapsburg became extinct with the Emperor Charles VI. in 1720. By virtue of the monarchical arrangement, it claimed to have perpetuated itself through the marriage of Maria-Theresa, heiress of the Hapsburgs, with Francis Duke of Lorraine and Bar. In 1735, by the Peace of Vienna, the Duke of Lorraine restored to France the states over which his race had ruled since 1038. In exchange he received the Grand Duchy of Tuscany, to which neither Austria nor Lorraine had a shadow of right, but which would shortly be vacant owing to the imminent demise of Jean-Gaston de Médicis, last of his race.

Francis of Lorraine was married in 1736, became Grand Duke of Tuscany in 1737, and was elected and crowned Emperor of Germany in 1745. He had an imposing family by Maria-Theresa, consisting of five sons and eleven daughters. His son Leopold II. also had sixteen children by Marie-Louise of Spain, and his eldest son Francis, who succeeded in 1792 as Francis II., had ten by his second wife Maria-Theresa, daughter of Ferdinand I. of Naples and Sicily.

Blemishes abounded on the side of the Sicilian Bourbons, and this family, which spread the germs of tuberculosis throughout all the royal races allied to it, did not spare the House of Austria. The latter in addition bore the unmistakable signs of degeneration, multiplied and stereotyped by a succession of consanguineous marriages, until the hereditary type, persisting through the centuries, became the hall-mark of the race.

What, then, were its intellectual characteristics? It has been said that "The physical likeness was accompanied by an intellectual affinity of tastes, interests, and ambitions that lasted for centuries" (Dr. Galippe). The cause of this banal influence may perhaps be sought in the inflexible system to which all the princes and princesses of this House were subjected from their birth. Nor was this all. Their education was inseparably bound up with a religious discipline that crushed and suppressed all freedom of thought, along with the polyglot instruction that tended to obscure ideas by an infinite multiplication of forms of expression ; for, the more varied the words into which thought is translated, the less clear does the thought become. This religious compulsion multiplied observances and devotions without appeal to conscience, nor did it inculcate any moral obligation or sense of human responsibility in these princes. The exercise of individual thought was stunted, and all activity absorbed in the performance of minute daily duties ; this, with absolute subordination to the Imperial Order, formed the basis of the family government. So long as they yielded strict submission the Arch-Dukes received titles and great possessions; they might command armies if they had the requisite genius. But here again they owed obedience to the Aulic Council which represented the Emperor, and if they sought to emancipate themselves were crushed without regard to their position or reputation.

The Austrian Court, while the most sumptuous, was also the simplest in Europe. When it had a mind to make a display, its pomp equalled the magnificence of an Oriental potentate. Four supreme departments, each with a directive administration under the immediate orders of the respective Grand Dignitaries, controlled thousands of officials. That of the Premier Grand Master of the Court, *e.g.*, comprised the offices of the Grand Master of the Kitchen, Grand Master of the Plate, Grand Steward of the Household, Director-General of Court Buildings, Prefect of the Library, Superintendent of the Band, Grand Master of the Ceremonies; it controlled the German, Hungarian, and Italian Guards of Nobles as well as the Traban

Guards and the Palace Guard of whom the Premier Grand Master was Colonel ; it was responsible for the Court Chapel, also for the medical and financial departments, and for the superintendence of the furniture, gardens, menagerie, and counting-house. In like manner, the Grand Chamberlain, Grand Marshal, and Grand Equerry each controlled a corresponding number of appointments. This Court was sumptuously apparelled. The uniforms were of the utmost magnificence, and the national costumes were adorned with diamonds and precious stones. The style of the garments, the splendour of the materials, the choice furs, tall head-dresses, and brilliant arms, rivalled the magnificence of adjacent Turkey.

Along with this, nothing could be simpler, more ordinary, more *bourgeois* than the habitual daily life of the Sovereign and the princes of his House. When he went out the Emperor took neither suite, nor guards, nor escort, and his relaxation in an existence which was regulated to the minute, consisted in the practice of some handicraft such as making sealing-wax, in despatching official letters, or in a visit at fixed hours to some obscure or impecunious mistress. The princesses of the blood were brought up under the direction of a governess or aja, who was charged with the superintendence of their household, the arrangement of their occupations, and the supervision of their tasks and instruction in the languages spoken within and without the Monarchy. They led a secluded and cloistered existence, and only females were kept in their bird-cages and dog-kennels. Their

reading was censored as well as their correspondence ;
music alone was permissible, and formed their main
diversion.

These princesses, however, constituted the reserve
corps of the Monarchy. With indisputable skill the
Emperor kept it at full strength, and was ever ready
to mobilise it. After defeating Austria in the War of
the Succession, the House of Bourbon believed it held
the mastery of Europe by reason of France, Spain,
Naples, and Parma, and that it was only necessary to
unite these four Powers in a close alliance—the Family
Compact. This was accomplished, and it was imagined
in France that the sacrifice of so much blood and the
heavy costs justified the issue. Austria, however,
weary of useless wars, disposed of three of her daughters
to Versailles, Naples, and Parma, which sufficed to
dissolve the Family Compact, to sever the alliances,
to embroil Madrid and Versailles, to pour the royal
treasures into Austria's empty coffers, and to render
abortive all the combinations which aimed at annexa-
tion of the Austrian Low Countries or resistance to
the projects of the Queen of the Two Sicilies. Austria
took her revenge by means of three or four of Maria-
Theresa's daughters, and under the most astonishing
misapprehension, the Governments (blind to the
hereditary blemishes, to feminine ambition, to the
anti-dynastic, anti-national influence of these women)
accepted as gospel the statement of Maria-Theresa
that her children were *moules à enfants*, who brought
to the countries they honoured by their advent a
reserve which would restrain them in politics, an

economy which they would apply consistently, a harmony of virtues which would make them good mothers, good wives, and good sovereigns. They contrived to be Arch Duchesses of Austria, and for Austria that sufficed.

In 1809, vanquished Austria was seeking to take her revenge. The procedure which had been successful half a century ago would serve her turn again. It was only necessary to fix the price.

In 1809, the Emperor Francis, second of the name in Lorraine, second in Germany, first in Austria, had been reigning seventeen years. He ascended the throne on the death of his father, Leopold II., and had made perpetual war upon France since 1790, upon Napoleon since 1796. The Emperor did not accompany his armies, but gambled by proxy and lost every throw. The Low Countries, Lombardy, the Brisgau, the left bank of the Rhine were his first stake ; Tuscany and the rights over Italy as a whole, the second ; the Venetian States, Tyrol and the Empire of Germany itself, the third ; Carnolia, Trieste, Friuli, Carinthia, Galicia, and Dalmatia, the fourth ; besides the war subsidies, and the occupation of most of his States by the military who might be cheery boon companions, but were none the less avaricious and out for pillage. The Emperor had instigated the campaigns and had declared war upon four occasions in the name of Austria-Hungary. He seldom took direct responsibility, but lent his name to the syndicate composed of all the enemies of revolutionary France. Consider what that syndicate stood for ; what hatred smouldered beneath it, what strings it pulled, what relations it established. It controlled cabinets, armies, and nations ; its aim was to counter revolutionary movements, to organise secret societies in the service of the autocracy, to train individuals linked to the Empire by ties of which they ignored the strength to promote the uprising of Europe against her masters, for thus only could it compass the fall of Napoleon. The *raison d'être* of this syndicate (quartered in Vienna rather than in London, whither flocked second-rate diplomatists, professional spies, deserters from the French army, adventurers from all over the world) was its hatred of France, so that on each occasion when she flared up, this syndicate of oligarchs promptly did its utmost to bring about civil war.

Its most recent enterprise had not been successful. Adopting the procedure of the enemy by enrolling in their service the forces it utilised, and by taking advantage of the most opportune moment, the oligarchs had this time risked all and lost everything. The Empire of Germany, degraded into the Empire of Austria, became a phantasm. Hungary, indeed, remained, for when Napoleon at one moment thought of annexing her, he feared the dynastic fidelity which had declared with such enthusiasm for " King Maria-Theresa." By a strange monarchical bias, he had abstained from erasing this name from the map of Europe, just as, two years previously, he had permitted Prussia to live and to recuperate her forces in the anticipation of some successful perfidy. No power accepts defeat, unless it renounces its claim to be a nation. Austria was at this time nothing but a fortuitous grouping of States, but the syndicate that governed her maintained an illusory life and activity. So long as the syndicate governed, so long as the sovereign reigned or believed that he reigned, the one would seek revenge, the other would cover it with his name. But they resolved to alter their methods. There had been enough of wars and battles, enough of conspiracies and projected assassinations. Gentler methods should be resorted to :

Bella gerant alii, tu felix Austria nube.

Napoleon was just then seeking a wife, and his advances had met with no encouragement in Russia, where he had felt sure of a favourable answer. Elsewhere, in Bavaria, for example, he met with no encouragement, but in Vienna his proposals were acceded to with incredible servility. The eldest daughter of the late Empress Maria-Theresa of Bourbon-Sicily had attained the age of eighteen on December 12, 1809. She had no claim to beauty, but was all that could be desired as the incarnation of the House of Austria. She was an attractive girl, fair and fresh with a very white skin, tinged with red, and pitted with small-pox. Her figure was well developed, her hands and feet were abnormally small, her mouth and chin were symbolical, as representing the race of Marie of Burgundy and Philippe le Beau, a mouth and chin which proclaim the degeneration of a perishing race, decimated by tuberculosis, mania, and imbecility. But what appears to modern science

as the fatal brand of a decadent race, was then
regarded as the stamp of illustrious origin. The
features of Marie-Louise-Léopoldine-Caroline-Lucie
were moulded upon those of her father, the Emperor ;
she possessed the grossly heavy pendulous lip, the
hall-mark of this House. A woman who observed
her closely remarked, "Her nose is hollowed at the
root, the lips and lower part of the face are thick
and somewhat heavy, the teeth are white but rather
far apart and slightly tilted forwards, the neck is
large but fine, the shoulders beautiful, hands pretty,
arms fine though somewhat red, feet pretty, height
five feet two inches, in other respects a fine woman."

As the eldest daughter, at the age of two, after
some childish maladies and an attack of small-pox
which marked her permanently, she was given a
Household, which, in accordance with the custom
imported from Madrid, necessitated an Aja, or Grand
Mistress, an appointment which was not, as might be
supposed, superior to political considerations, but
was even dependent on them. Accordingly, Marie-
Louise had three governesses before 1805. One of
these, who exercised an undoubted influence upon her,
was a Frenchwoman, *née* Folliot de Crenneville, who,
after marrying a Baron de Pontet, Colonel of a Wal-
loon Regiment, had accompanied him to Vienna.
Her husband died, so by intrigue and *savoir-faire* she
succeeded in 1799 in wedding Comte Colloredo-
Walsee, Minister of State, Imperial Chancellor and
Grand Master of the Emperor's Court when he was
Arch-Duke and heir apparent. She thus established

herself down to 1805 in her great office, and although she was deprived of it after Austerlitz by political vicissitudes, her influence over her pupil, who remained constantly faithful to her, was undiminished.

Madame de Colloredo shared the opinions which were in vogue at the Court of Vienna ; those of the Princess of the Two Sicilies who was its Empress, likewise of the Emperor, of the courtiers and of the entire people ; naturally the Imperial Princess was precluded from holding any other views. These she expresses in her correspondence with her aja and with the daughter of the latter, Mlle. de Pontet, who, on April 1, 1810, became Comtesse de Crenneville, by her marriage with her uncle.

In these letters we find sentiments that could not have been pretence, but which are the true expression of the mind of Marie-Louise. On September 8, 1803, she wrote :

" Maman [Mme. de Colloredo] has made me write down the title of a book she wishes to obtain from France, which she believes will be suitable for us. It is the *Plutarque de la Jeunesse*, by the same Blanchard who wrote the two works we have already perused. It is the life of illustrious men, from Homer to Buonaparte. This name tarnishes his work, and I would have preferred that he had concluded with Francis II.,* who has also performed remarkable feats in re-establishing the Theresianum, etc., etc., whereas the other has committed nothing but in-

* As this letter was written on September 8, 1803, Marie-Louise gives her father his title of Emperor of Germany.

justice by depriving certain people of their countries.
. . . Maman has just told me of an amusing incident.
M. Buonaparte, when in Egypt, was saved with only
two or three other persons at the time his army was
routed, and became a Turk ; that is, he said to the
Turks ' I am not your enemy, I am a Musulman, I
accept the Great Mahomet as prophet.' Afterwards,
on returning to France, he professed himself the
Catholic which he really is. Then only was he
raised to the dignity of Consul. . . . It is not for me
to judge, but I think it is profaning our Holy Religion
to say that one belongs to another, for the Credo
states one ought to confess one's faith."

Here we get to the root of the matter. Marie-
Louise was then fourteen, and that is the kind of
history she was taught. Two years later what she
knew of Napoleon was on the same lines : " You will
already be aware," she wrote to Victoire de Pontet,
" what a snub Monsieur Champagny has received,
for of all the Ministers, Talleyrand alone has been
excepted ; so it is said. The Corsican sent for
Champagny and asked him brusquely why he had
always concealed from him the belligerent sentiments
of the House of Austria. Champagny replied : ' It
was because I did not know you would take the Crown
of Italy.' Thereupon a resounding smack on the face
was M. de Champagny's reward."

When the *débâcle* came and the Imperial Princes
and Princesses were obliged to fly before the French,
such fictions availed them little. In fact, on November
15, 1805, " Their Majesties the Emperor Francis and

his wife the Empress Marie-Thérèse, simultaneously dismissed Count Colloredo, Minister of the Cabinet, and Countess Colloredo, Aja to the Arch-Duchess."

This palace revolution for the moment suppressed political reflections, but when the war recommenced under the influence of the new Empress Maria-Ludovica of Este, not only was there no change of attitude, but the animosity burned more fiercely than before. This is seen in the account of the Battle of Essling, where, when confronted with the Arch-Duke Charles, waving the banner of the Grenadiers, "The French took to their heels and abandoned Napoleon who cried after them that he would burn them with the bridge, and with his own hand slew two of his guards." What a triumph! "It is the first time Napoleon has been beaten in person. He has lost 22,000 men and 16,000 wounded have been transported to Vienna." And, at Buda, people were flocking to the Orczy Garden to see the "Half-rotted and naked French float by." The Arch-Duchess concluded: "I have already on several occasions been tempted to believe that we are approaching the end of the world, and that he who oppresses us is Anti-Christ." The French were to be punished in their turn, for, "Verily, by their cruelties and sacrileges, they draw down the malediction of Heaven. They cast priests into the flames, fling away the consecrated wafers to steal the pyx, and trample them under foot."

Now, however, came a truce. Bubna had been sent to congratulate Napoleon on his birthday. "I am sure," wrote Marie-Louise, "that he will send his

congratulations to Mamma [the Empress Maria-
Ludovica] on her name-day. . . . I assure you that
to see this creature would be for me a worse torture
than all the martyrdoms, and I am not sure that this
is not what he has in his mind."

The horror Marie-Louise had conceived of the
French and of Napoleon seems to have possessed her
as it did the entire Austrian Court. At the beginning
of the year 1810 the rumour spread that Napoleon
was separated from Joséphine and was seeking
another bride. Marie-Louise heard of it from Kosse-
luch, her professor of music. She wrote on January
10 to Mlle. de Pontet: "I see him talking about the
separation of Napoleon from his wife. I even have
an idea that he thinks of me as her successor, but in
this he is mistaken, for Napoleon is too much afraid
of a refusal, and too anxious to do us more mischief,
to make any such request, and Papa is too kind to
constrain me on a point of such importance." On
the same day she wrote to Madame de Colloredo : " I
let every one talk and am not the least disturbed by
it. I only pity the unfortunate princess he will choose,
for I am certain it will not be I who am to become the
victim of politics." Ten days later, she began to grow
uneasy, and wrote : " Since Napoleon's divorce, I open
every *Frankfort Gazette* with the idea of finding news
of the nomination of the new wife, and I admit that
this delay causes me involuntary uneasiness. I leave
my fate in the hands of Divine Providence who alone
knows what can make us happy ; but, should misfortune so decree, I am ready to sacrifice my individual

happiness to the good of the State, being persuaded that true happiness can only be found in the accomplishment of one's duties even to the prejudice of one's inclinations. I will think of it no more, but if it has to be, my mind is made up notwithstanding it will be a double and very painful sacrifice. Pray for me, that it may not be so!" Notwithstanding this resignation it can hardly be said that the Arch-Duchess accepted the cup. She wrote on the 23rd: "I know at Vienna they are already marrying me to the *Great Napoleon:* I hope it will end in talk . . . and should it come about I believe I shall be the only one who will not rejoice at it. . . ."

In the House of Austria, the Princesses were not consulted. They were brought up to realise that marriage for them was entirely a matter of expediency, inseparable from the politics of the House. Usually speaking, however, the Princes in question were on an equality, whereas in this case the wooer was a *parvenu*—"*Le Parvenu Corse.*" No matter! When the Emperor shall invoke the higher interests of the Dynasty, Marie-Louise will say, like her sister Leopoldine at the moment of her departure to wed the Emperor of Brazil: "I confess that the sacrifice of leaving my family, and that perhaps for ever, will be very painful to me, but this alliance gratifies my father, and in separating myself from him, I shall have the consolation of knowing that I have conformed to his wishes, being persuaded that Providence directs our fate as princesses in a special way, and that we are obeying its will in submitting to that of our parents."

More brutally, Metternich said : " Our princesses
are rarely accustomed to choose their husbands
according to the affections of their heart, and the
respect paid to the will of her father by a child so
good and well brought up as the Arch-Duchess,
makes me hope that we shall encounter no obstacle
on her side."

When the marriage had been finally decided on
by Imperial policy, no objection could be admitted ;
for the rest, none was made either by the Emperor or
by his daughter.

It was from the courier who bore her marriage-
contract signed by Schwarzenberg that the Arch-
Duchess learned all at once that she had been asked,
promised, and bestowed, and that she was about to
be handed over. Nor was it even her father who
warned her of the imminence of the sacrifice to be
exacted from her. It was Metternich, who having
sought an interview with the Emperor, remarked :
" Sire, occasions occur in the life of States as in that
of individuals, in which a third person cannot put
himself in the place of the one responsible for the
decision to be taken. . . . Your Majesty is Sovereign
and Father ; you alone can properly be consulted in
regard to your duties as Father and Emperor."
Whereupon the Emperor remarked : " I leave the
decision to my daughter, for I would never constrain
her. I desire before taking my duties as Sovereign
into consideration, to know what she intends to do.
Go and seek the Arch-Duchess, and bring me word
what she has said to you." Undoubtedly he knew

what he could count on. At Buda, when he had
spoken to his daughter of a necessary sacrifice, he
had known she would bow to it, therefore he had
summoned her a few days previously to Vienna, so
that she might be ready at hand.

" What does my father wish ? " inquired the Arch-
Duchess of Metternich, to which, when the Minister
assured her that she was entirely free to say what she
wished, she declared : " I desire only what my duty
commands me to desire. When the interests of the
Empire are in question they must be considered, and
not my wish. Entreat my father to do only his duty
as Sovereign and not to subordinate it to my personal
interest." When Metternich reported these words to
the Emperor, he replied : " What you say does not
surprise me, I know my daughter too well not to have
anticipated a similar reply. I have employed the
time you passed with her in making my decision.
My consent to this marriage will secure to the
Monarchy some years of political peace which I can
devote to healing its wounds. I owe entire consideration for the happiness of my people, therefore I must
not hesitate."

The sacrifice once resolved on, nothing further had
to be taken into consideration, neither the Revolution,
nor the death of Marie Antoinette, nor the origin of
the Corsican's family ; not his habits, nor his manners,
nor the way in which he beat his Ministers and killed
his Generals. Nothing mattered beyond securing to
the Monarchy some years of political peace. Surely
it might be inferred from this observation of the

Emperor, that Austria had now formulated her plans, and in thus gaining a reprieve which would permit her to recuperate her forces, she would, when the day arrived, resume her intentions which had been four times interrupted, and deliver a new and decisive assault ?

But what about the Arch-Duchess ? Are we to suppose that she was in the plot, that her father had imparted to her projects of which he was not yet fully cognisant ?

He saw a means of gaining time, of securing for himself a few years in order that he might, if occasion arose, resume operations against France, but was not certain either of the time or the opportunity. In Europe every State was in the same plight. The letters of Alexander of Russia to his mother, the Empress Marie-Feodorovna, prove that he never acted in good faith after Tilsit ; and even after Erfurt he did not fling himself into the combat, though he refused to take advantage of the Spanish successes, and though a little later on he seemed almost to be faithful to the French Alliance, it was still the same story. He refused to sacrifice his sister ; did he, or was it the Empress Mother ?

Napoleon, on his side, saw in this marriage the consummation of his amazing fortune. He, the son of a Clerk of the Records in Corsica, who had died in debt and almost insolvent; he, the exhibitioner of Brienne, the Jacobin General who had destroyed the Royalists at Toulon and had crushed them in Paris ; who in Italy and Egypt had carried pillage and devastation along his track ; he was now on the eve of wedding a daughter of the House of Austria. The consideration that he was already married, and that the attitude he had adopted in regard to his first wife indicated that he reserved a privileged place for her alongside the second, had been of no more weight than the legends with which his life was surrounded. The canons of the Church, and the prescriptions of religious marriage, had gone by the board. He came, he saw, he conquered ! Every point had been yielded and he was to come into possession. He reviewed it all. He was genuinely elated by the magnificence of the union he was about to contract ; he handled it, held it, and realized in it all the splendour of the alliances it procured and the consummated entry into the Family of the Kings. He would no longer be the *parvenu* who had carved for himself an Empire out of the ancient Monarchies by force of arms ; who brought in his train brothers and sisters, a babbling crowd of women with their lovers, and men with their mistresses, a horde of new-comers, devoid of genius, talent, and still more of distinction. He was now making his position secure, consolidating it, and uniting it with the most ancient tradition of which Europe could boast, for he would become simultaneously a Bourbon and a Hapsburg. He saw himself as the nephew of Louis XVI. and of Marie-Antoinette, the great-nephew of Louis the XIV. and Maria-Theresa. He would assume the glory, the achievement of centuries, acquired only by the labour of generations, which he had attained after ten years of victory, of struggle, and the reconstruction of France; all these, indeed, had failed to carry him to the summit, but this marriage would establish him there. He hastened to secure his prize.

As soon as Schwarzenberg's courier was on the road to Vienna, Napoleon began to organise and arrange, not forgetting to make provision for his children! The trousseau and marriage gifts must be dispatched from Paris, nothing was to be purchased in Vienna. The dowry allotted to Marie-Antoinette, Queen of France, was inadequate for Marie-Louise, the Empress. The Empress must have four millions. His eldest son will be the King of Rome : true, the last to bear this title was the Emperor Francis, King of the Romans, but what of that ? Of what account is the title of King of Rome to him, when he has lost the Holy Romano-Germanic Empire ? Should it not revert to Napoleon, who is in possession of the city of Rome and the patrimony allocated by the Emperor Charles V. to the Holy Father ? Is it enough to have provided for one son ? Must there not be a throne for the younger brother ? So Eugène, deprived of the promised succession to the Kingdom of Italy (the stipulated condition of his marriage), was reduced to the inheritance of the Grand-Duchy of Frankfort. Napoleon contented himself with providing for two boys ; due credit must be allowed for his moderation.

As soon as the courier returned from Vienna with the assent of Marie-Louise, the news was officially announced to the Emperor's family ; it was communicated to the Senate, and made the occasion of sports and *fêtes*. Berthier, Prince de Neuchâtel and Prince de Wagram, was dispatched to ask for the hand of the Arch-Duchess at Vienna, and to bring back the new Iphigenia in all haste. Napoleon's impatience was so great that he would not allow his companion in arms to display his taste for luxury and his " yellow magnificence." * Berthier was bidden to take a limited suite of some sixteen servants and no State carriages. The Household of the Empress was appointed ; the Duchesse de Montebello (widow of the hero slain at Essling) was selected to be lady-in-waiting in place of Mme. de La Rochefoucauld, who was superannuated. The other ladies had all formed part of Josephine's Household ; but the grand *rôle* was not on this occasion allotted to the lady-in-waiting. This position had to be reserved for a near relative of the Emperor, some one possessing dignity, activity, and decision. Elisa was out of the question for this office of Superintendent of the Household ; she had the requisite intelligence, but not sufficient dignity ; Pauline was impossible ; as were also the sisters-in-law, Julie and Hortense ; Catherine was too young and inexperienced, though she alone would have the traditions, the breeding, and the manners, but she was unsuited to the post. Caroline, the youngest of Napoleon's sisters, alone remained ; ambitious, thirsting for honours, infatuated with etiquette, intelligent, dominating, full of enterprise and perseverance, she was capable of carrying out the most difficult missions.

---

* Berthier had a passion for yellow, which he displayed in his livery, his carriages, and even in the uniform of his soldiers.

She knew her own mind, and nothing could make her yield nor bend. She might be lacking in formalities and graces and thus offend the Princess whose first responsibilities were to be confided to her ; but on points of ceremonial no concession would be made, the Emperor's orders would be punctually executed, and the Austrian Court would have only what was due to it and nothing more. Much indeed could be said against the appointment. Caroline had had more than one *liaison*, and every one at Court knew that she was on the best of terms with Metternich ; a more serious drawback was the fact that she occupied the throne of Marie-Louise's grandmother at Naples, and that in fulfilling for the Empress the part allotted under Marie-Antoinette to the Princesse de Lamballe, she might acquire undue influence, and establish herself as directress. The fact, however, that she would be compelled to spend much of her time at Naples, made the risk of such ascendancy very small, also there was Madame de Montebello to be reckoned with.

At first this lady, whether because she had determined from that time to submit to no authority that might interfere with her, or because she entertained a strong antipathy to the Emperor on personal grounds, or because she took no interest in the matter and from this very fact acquired an irresistible influence over a young girl craving to be loved, did not appear at the outset to have any desire for domination. She had been Mademoiselle Guéhéneue, the daughter of a senator, and bore a name of great

distinction after her marriage—that of a Marshal of
the Empire, the most faithful of the Emperor's
companions, the best soldier, and the only marshal
hitherto slain on the field of battle. But in spite of
this she had neither the education, nor the good
manners, still less the character for such a post. She
was pretty, and she knew it, but she was amiable only
towards her friends. They received all her favours
and were only two or three in number: Corvisart,
the physician, and an equerry, M. de Saint-Aignan;
none were women. She liked to withdraw with her
children to live a solitary life in her château at
Maisons, in her house in the rue d'Enfer, or even in a
more distant estate inherited from her parents. She
had a mania for bibelots of every kind, porcelain,
bronzes, jewels, fans, she collected everything, coveted
everything, and acquired it. After her death, the sale
of her effects continued for weeks at her house.

It should have been Madame de Montebello's duty
to whisper suggestions in the Empress's ear, as
to words, phrases, graces, social hints, and all those
considerations which Josephine had so tactfully
employed towards every one, but Marie-Louise cared
little for these things and Madame de Montebello even
less. She disdained and despised all who were not of
her own set. She hated the Emperor, who had not
made her a Princess like Madame Davout or Madame
Massena, not that the title would have rendered her
more assiduous in her duties, or more concerned with
the mysteries of etiquette. She had no memory, nor
did she trouble to cultivate one. So much the worse

if she blundered over names ; if they aspired to be illustrious what did that matter to the Empress ?

Marie-Louise was shy, and haughty, but seeing she was encouraged in this at every turn, how should she be otherwise ?

Madame de Luçay, who was Mistress of the Robes, might have acquired some influence had Marie-Louise been a coquette and shown a little taste in the manner of adorning herself, instead of restricting the choice of her gowns to definite colours in consequence of being constantly dominated by the idea of keeping within her allowance. But Madame de Luçay was bound hand and foot by etiquette. In the first place, she was preoccupied with the frequent illness of her gouty husband, also with her daughter and son-in-law Segur, besides which she was over-awed by the Emperor, who was for her the embodiment of wisdom. She was of no account and the ladies of the Palace even less so.

Whether they were Josephine's former ladies, or were nominated in consequence of being nearer in age to the new Empress, they did not appear, and when etiquette required their presence they behaved like a dumb-show, seeming barely to exist. Some of them, coquettes desirous of playing a part, might win a glance from the Emperor which was lucrative ; that was all, she was and she would be just Madame de Montebello and nothing more. From the very first day of the arrival of the Prince Vice-Constable at Vienna, all passed off as was intended, including the visits, the presentations, the receptions, the *fauteuils*, the speeches, the gestures, the amazing cortège which accompanied Berthier to the Burg as he issued from the Schwarzenberg Palace outside the Carinthian Gate, whither the Grand Marshal of the Court had proceeded with great pomp to fetch him. Owing to rigorous discipline this most sumptuous and magnificent pageant moved by word of command with the silence of a regiment, for every gesture had been regulated with mechanical precision.

Headed by a detachment of cavalry, in advance of three grooms on horseback in gala livery, the State coach of the Privy Councillors and Chamberlains was followed by a second State carriage drawn by six horses containing the Ambassador's secretary with his Master of the Ceremonies and the Steward of the Court. Liveried footmen, running grooms, and the Grand Marshal's lackeys followed in the liveries of the Ambassador of France. Then appeared six horses drawing the State carriage of the Ambassador and Grand Marshal, attended by two of the Emperor's footmen in gala livery at the doors, together with three major-domos of the Palace mounted, and the Ambassador's equerry and aides-de-camp; then followed two outriders with the second equerry of the Ambassador, after which three carriages, each drawn by six horses, followed one another containing the officials (*cavaliers*) of the Embassy with officers of the Ambassador's Household, attended by outriders. The procession terminated with a detachment of cavalry.

After his reception by the Prince of Zinzendorff

the Ambassador, accompanied by the Grand Marshal, entered the Palace followed by his entire household and passed between the ranks of Grenadiers, Palace Guards, Musketeers, and the Hungarian Guard of Nobles. His flunkeys he left in the Traban Hall, the officers of his household in the Hall of the Gentlemen, and the Embassy officials between the two first columns of the great new hall. On finding himself in the presence of the Emperor, who stood beneath a canopy with his head covered, Berthier bared his head, bowing three times. The Emperor did not uncover until after the first salutation, and replaced his hat immediately. The Ambassador delivered his speech with his head covered, but removed its covering each time he pronounced the name of one of the two Sovereigns, and whenever the name of the Emperor Napoleon was mentioned, the Emperor Francis saluted.

The impress of the Revolution was seen at the Grand Banquet which took place in the Empress' apartments, when for the first time the humble folk, not accredited with thirty-two quarterings, were admitted and received. At the costume ball which followed the repast, held in the *salons* of the Imperial Redoubt, six thousand persons were present : some, like Prince Esterhazy, covered with diamonds. Lejeune, one of Berthier's gentlemen, challenged Esterhazy to the first duel, and Esterhazy promised him to wear this dress ; what amenities !

On March 8 the suit was preferred. In his speech to the Emperor Francis, Berthier remarked :

" The eminent qualities for which this Princess is distinguished have destined her for a place upon a great throne. She will thus ensure the happiness of a great People and that of a great man." To which the Austrian simply replied : " I grant the hand of my daughter to the Emperor of the French."

The Arch-Duchess, accompanied by her Grand Mistress and Grand Master, was thereupon presented by the Grand Chamberlain. Having approached her father with a deep curtsey and bowed to the Ambassador, she took her seat on the Emperor's left. Berthier made another speech as he handed the portrait of Napoleon to the Arch-Duchess, meanwhile holding a letter in his hand. This is the letter :

" *Madame ma sœur*, the success of the suit that I have preferred to H.M. the Emperor your father, to unite myself with you in marriage, is a very precious indication of the esteem and consideration he bestows on me. I am deeply touched by the consent that you on your part give to a union that consummates for me the greatest joy and which should adorn my whole life. . . . I have charged the Prince de Neuchâtel, my Ambassador Extraordinary and Plenipotentiary, to deliver to you my portrait. I beg you to receive it as a gage of the sentiments which are graven on my heart and which will be unalterable."

To the phrase, " It is above all from your heart, Madame, that the Emperor my Master desires to obtain you," Marie-Louise replied : " With the

permission of my father I give my consent to my
union with the Emperor Napoleon." She thereupon
desired her governess to affix the Emperor's portrait
to her breast.

The reserve of the Austrians contrasted with the
phrases of the Bergers de Lignon,* which seemed so
out of place in the mouth of the conquerors. After
conclusion of such formalities as the solemn renunciation of the Austrian Succession, confirmation of the
Pragmatic Sanction and the Order of Succession, the
oath was taken before the crucifix ; followed at the
Grand Theatre, in presence of the Emperor and
Empress together with the Arch-Duchess, the Ambassador and his whole suite, by a representation of
Iphigénie en Aulide, by Gluck. The marriage contract, involving delivery of the dowry of 400,000
francs in gold ducats enclosed in a coffer, followed.
This caused the Archbishop of Vienna to raise his
timid protest, seeing that the Austrian Court recognised neither the major excommunication fulminated
by the Pope, June 11, 1809, nor the reservation by
the Holy See in regard to annulment of marriages
among sovereigns ; but the certificate of the Ambassador of France having been held sufficient, all was
ready and nothing remained but to proceed with the
marriage. It would be solemnised on the 11th, which
was a Sunday, the only day of the week in Lent on
which it was permissible to celebrate.

The cortège, which was marshalled in the apart-

* Characters in *L'Astrée*, a pastoral play of the seventeenth century,
to which allusions abound in the French literature of the period.

ments, passed through the Augustinian Cloister, draped with green cloth, in order to reach the church. In order of precedence with majestic array, the Prince de Neuchâtel preceded the Arch-Dukes who walked two and two, until the last before the Emperor was the Arch-Duke Charles, whom Napoleon had nominated to represent himself at the nuptial ceremony. After the Emperor the Empress was seen leading the *fiancée*.

Complication arose during the ceremonial celebrated according to the ritual of Vienna in the German tongue, in consequence of a stranger, who was not a King, having been admitted during the Imperial Banquet to the Emperor's table for the first time.

It was on the 13th that the Empress of the French set out on her journey. Escorted in her carriage by Arch-Duke Charles between two ranks of soldiers, at a walking pace, she traversed the streets of Vienna filled by a saddened, almost indignant crowd. The cannon thundered, the bells clashed, Marie-Louise arrived at Saint-Polton whither the Emperor had gone with all the Imperial family. There, on the 13th of the month, was held the last dinner, the last *soirée*. Next morning after Mass the new Empress took leave of her father.

The handing over was to be accomplished at Braunau. The retinue with which Marie-Louise was to arrive after having halted on the 14th at Ems in the Palace of the Prince of Auersperg and on the 15th at Ried, consisted of eighty-three carriages or waggons together with four hundred and fifty-three

draught-horses and eight saddle horses. Besides the
Grand Masters and Grand Mistresses there were
twelve ladies of the Palace, twelve Chamberlains, and
a detachment of the Hungarian Guard of Nobles;
the *personnel* exceeded three hundred dignitaries.

The handing over did not actually take place at
Braunau, for the town contained no suitable premises;
consequently the engineers of the French army, in
occupation since 1809, had put up temporary buildings
divided into three halls (French, Neutral, and Austrian);
two entrances led up to the building, one on the
Braunau side (typifying France) and the other towards Altheim (for Austria). Nothing had been
omitted from its luxurious appointments, and stoves
distributed an agreeable warmth through the rooms.
Avenues planted with green trees gave a permanent
aspect to this temporary construction. Having left
Ried at eight in the morning of the 16th, the Empress
arrived at Altheim at eleven, where she divested herself of her travelling garments and reached the
temporary buildings at two o'clock. The French
had been awaiting her in their halls for an hour and
a half in gala costume. Having rested in the
Austrian hall she passed into the central hall, where
her Court assembled round her. The French Court
now entered and took up its position opposite the
Austrian Court. The Acts of handing over and
Reception were read and the signatures appended
and sealed. The Austrian cortège took leave with
tears as they kissed the hand of their Arch-Duchess.
after which the Austrian Commissary gave the hand

of the Empress to the French Commissary. Caroline made her *entrée*, embraced Marie-Louise, and welcomed her.

There was yet another ceremony with the Arch-Duke Antoine, who had been sent by the Emperor of Austria to compliment the Queen of Naples, so they took carriages for Braunau, seven in number. That of the Empress having eight white horses, surrounded by grooms and pages on horseback, kept in the centre of the cortège, which defiled between the Friant, Padone, and Pajol Divisions, amid salutes from the officers with banners, cannons firing a salvo, and trumpets sounding. They arrived at Braunau, where a palace had been constructed by breaking through the walls of two houses.

The trousseau was exhibited by the Lady of the Bedchamber. Marie-Louise, whose hair and dress were now arranged *à la française*, received the homage of her ladies and officers of her household.

Before the departure of Count von Trauttmansdorff, who had charge of the handing over, the Empress entrusted to him the last letter she was able to write freely to her father. "I think of you continually, and I shall always think of you. God has given me strength to bear this last shock courageously. In Him alone I place all my confidence. He will help me and will give me courage, and I shall find calm in the resolution to fulfil my duty to you, since I have made you this sacrifice." She then described her emotions at being separated from all her ladies, except Countess Lazinkska, her Grand Mistress,

whom Napoleon had promised to leave near her, and
who before the end of the week would be sent back
to Vienna : she mentioned the " icy shudder that
fell upon her " and her repugnance to the French
women : " Oh God ! so different to the Viennese
ladies." Her feeling of insecurity with regard to
the Queen of Naples, to whom, however, she was
astonishingly amiable ; the ordeal of the two hours'
toilette, whence she emerged as perfumed as the
French women whose society during a long journey
she dreaded ; the discomfiture of not having yet
received a letter from Napoleon ; all these were
recorded.

Such were her thoughts at the moment when she
was entering on her new life, when she was about to
adopt at one and the same moment a husband and
the customs of a country, all unknown to her, and
hostile alike to her pride, her race, her past, in short
to everything that mattered to her !

CHAPTER III

IT may be instructive to consider for a moment the commissariat necessary for the retinue of the Empress when on tour. The following was the customary procedure in France according to Imperial etiquette, Royalty would have done otherwise. Some curtailment might possibly have been anticipated—but it was not.

The procession was divided into three parts. The first started twelve hours before her Majesty, headed by a Sub-Inspector of Posts with an outrider, preceding seven carriages, the first of which was a chariot drawn by six horses containing two ladies-in-waiting and a major-domo, having on the box a footman and a mechanic. The second, also a chariot with six horses, conveyed two chamberlains, an almoner, and a master of the ceremonies ; the third chariot, also drawn by six horses, contained a first woman of the chamber, a woman of the wardrobe, an usher and a valet de chambre, having a valet and a polisher on the box. The fourth carriage consisted of a landau drawn by four horses conveying a major-domo and a page having on the box the latter's footman, and followed by a caterer's cart in which rode a *maître d'hôtel*, an officer, and two cooks. After these followed a landau with four horses conveying two of the Ladies' waiting women; and lastly, a gondola with six horses for the servants of the personnel of the suite—38 horses and 2 hacks, together with 34 persons.

Her Majesty's cortège, preceded by an Equerry, a Sub-Inspector, an outrider, three under-grooms, comprised eight carriages: a chariot with six horses for the Lady-in-waiting, the Gentlemen-in-waiting, the first Equerry, a lady of the Court; on the box a footman and a mechanic. The Empress's carriage with six horses, coachman and footman on the box; a chariot with six horses for the Mistress of the Robes, a lady-in-waiting, two chamberlains; on the box a footman and a runner; two landaus with four horses for the equerries and the medical service; a chariot with six horses for the women, a caterer's cart for the commissariat, and a chariot for the Ladies' waiting-women—52 horses.

The third procession left six hours after the second, and included a landau for two pages, a landau for the valets-de-chambre, a waggon on springs with six horses for the wardrobe, a similar waggon with eight horses for the plate and china, a gondola for the servants—28 horses. Total, 120 horses levied from the country.

The equipage was organised with military precision. Each started by order from the equerry in charge of the departures, *e.g.* "Madame de K—— will accompany the procession which leaves the Tuileries on March 1, at five in the morning. She

will take her place in chariot No. 76 with Madame de
—— and MM. de ——. There will be half a valise
for two persons, a dressing case for each, to be fetched
and brought to the stables on the evening before the
departure, at eight o'clock. A place for a lady's-
maid in chariot No. 23."

The departure took place on the 17th, after Mass,
amid discharges of artillery. Braunau was reached
on the 9th. The Empress received congratulations
at Haag from the Prince of Bavaria, and at eight in
the evening reached Munich amid the firing of cannon
and pealing of bells, where the King and Queen of
Bavaria awaited her at the foot of the Palace stairs.
She supped alone with the Queen of Naples, and the
following day heard Mass at noon in the Throne-
room from her own apartment. Visits were exchanged, and just as the State dinner was about to be
commenced M. de Saint Aignan, Equerry to the
Emperor, arrived with the first letter from his
Master. The Queen of Naples, at the suggestion of
Madame de Montebello, thereupon pretended to have
received orders from her brother, and insisted that
Madame Lazinska should be sent back to Vienna.
Notwithstanding that the Emperor had written to
Count Otto on the 25th February, " There will be no
difficulty about a lady companion accompanying the
Empress during her journey ; I should even prefer a
lady companion to a waiting woman," Caroline
declared she had her orders. Nothing Austrian
should remain, not even the little Viennese lapdog,
her companion and last witness of the past. " The

Emperor," she said, " detests dogs, and will not allow
them in the Palace ; " the little animal therefore had
to go with Madame Lazinska, who took a plaintive
letter with her from the Empress in which she neither
accused the Emperor, for, as she said, " It is certainly
not his idea," nor did she blame Madame de Montebello who plotted the intrigue, but only the Queen
of Naples who dealt this double blow.

The royal dinner was followed by a performance
of Paër's *Achille*. On the morning of the 19th the
whole Bavarian Court was present at the Empress's
departure, which, notwithstanding she was tired and
really unwell owing to a cold, Caroline insisted on.
Luncheon was taken in Augsburg with the former
Elector of Trèves, and in the evening the Empress
arrived at Ulm, where the Grand Chamberlain of
Bavaria left her. A start was made at nine o'clock
on March 20. After having received congratulations
at the frontier of Wurtemburg, her Majesty reached
Stuttgart at half-past four, where the King and Queen
received her. She only spoke to the King, the Queen,
and the Princess Royal ; the Princes were not addressed. " These matters of etiquette are rather
extraordinary," wrote the King of Wurtemburg, but
he dared not complain. " At last ! " he exclaimed,
" it is all over."

Caroline, on the contrary, filled the Courts of
Germany with her lamentations. The King of
Wurtemburg wrote, " The poor Queen of Naples is
very tired, and, indeed, who would not be ? What
a task they have given her ! Really it is impossible.

D

She does her best, but I think she is somewhat tired of the post." How she had worked for this mission ! Having promised herself no small gain from it, neither trouble nor profit came amiss to her.

After dinner, the representation of a German opera, *The Judgment of Solomon,* was given. On the 21st they started at nine o'clock for Carlsruhe, which was reached at half-past five. The reception here was the same as at Munich and Stuttgart, save that the sons of the Hochberg did not appear at the dinner. After the presentations a performance of *Sargines,* an opera by Paër, was given.

Next day, the 22nd, the Empress was due to arrive in France, and after lunching at Rastadt, entered Strasbourg through streets green with trees, passing under a triumphal arch which had been erected at the extremity of the bridge, amid troops, garlands, and illuminations everywhere. But this was nothing in comparison with the rejoicings the following day. After Mass in the Imperial Palace, she received M. de Metternich, then the authorities presented by Madame de Luçay, woman of the chamber in the absence of Madame de Montebello, who did not appear during the halt at Strasbourg, owing to the body of her husband being buried there. From the balcony of the Palace, the Empress viewed the procession of the City Cor- porations as it passed along the terraces by the Ill, bearing the emblems of their trades or professions. At half-past three, she drove to the Robertsau and surveyed the guests at a banquet of seven to eight thousand persons, who drank her health. At eight in the evening she visited the Hôtel de la Préfecture, to witness a *fête* at which a cantata was rendered and a quadrille arranged for the most aristocratic of the young girls of the city. Amid the general illuminations that of the Spire, for which 50,000 lamps or cressets were employed, called forth general admiration, as also the illumination of an elevated set piece in front of the Palace, where three jets of water spouted forth amid thousands of lamps. On the 24th, at eight in the morning, the Prince de Neuchâtel sent a telegraphic dispatch to the Emperor announcing her departure : " Her Majesty is well and has a great desire to arrive speedily at Compiègne, but we are delayed by the enthusiasm of the towns. Her Majesty is much pleased with the city of Strasbourg." Thus the Empress expressed herself : " I beg you, dearest Papa, to pray earnestly for me. You may be sure that I shall make every effort to give you the consolation you expect from me."

Certainly, from the standpoint of ceremonial, nothing was omitted. In accordance with the Emperor's orders everything had been regulated, point by point, on the procedure employed for the marriage of Louis XVI., whom Napoleon now habitually referred to as " My predecessor," and occasionally as " My poor uncle." M. de Dreux-Brézé, Grand Master in 1789, was deferentially consulted. The Emperor noted the least incident and sent letters daily by M. de Beauvau to Stuttgart, by M. de Bondy to Carlsruhe, by Prince Corsini to Lunéville, by Maréchal Bessières to Nancy, not to mention the pheasants killed by his own hand, a piece of Royal gallantry, forwarded by pages.

Lejeune, aide-de-camp to the Prince de Neuchâtel, participated in all the ceremonies, for, being credited with talent as a painter, he was in favour with the Prince for whom he designed uniforms or liveries, and in like manner with the Emperor himself to whom he related Court gossip. He arrived at Compiègne with the Prince de Beauvau, who brought a letter from Marie-Louise. After giving audience to the Prince, the Emperor took Lejeune to his own room and demanded an account of all the ceremonies held at Vienna, Munich, and Stuttgart. With regard to the portrait of the Empress which he brought, Napoleon questioned Lejeune upon every detail of the likeness. Lejeune exhibited the profile he had sketched, and the Emperor at once exclaimed : "Ah ! that is indeed the Austrian lip of the Hapsburgs." Napoleon thereupon produced the medals of the Emperors which he compared with the portraits while detaining Lejeune over an hour. An outbreak of fire occurred at the top of the château, but he paid no attention to it. His whole mind was fixed on the reputed plainness which was the hall-mark of a race which placed in the hands of the conqueror not only Marie-Louise, but her entire lineage, enabling him to share in a long-established royalty. He holds it, he possesses it, and the whole of his past has vanished !

Meanwhile the Empress was approaching. Having left Strasbourg on the 24th at nine in the morning, she reached Saverne in time for lunch, and in the evening at six o'clock arrived at the Sous-Préfecture of Lunéville, where she dined. Next day, being Sunday, she started after Mass and breakfast, at eleven o'clock. At one o'clock she was at Nancy, where the Duc d'Istrie, on horseback, met her and handed her a letter from the Emperor. Napoleon sent her a brief note with his usual signature. On this occasion the letter "N" with which he signed it was 4½ centimetres high and 9 centimetres wide. The whole of his pride, his power, and realised ambition were in this letter "N"! It signified the height of his power and connoted his decadence and fall.

At four o'clock Marie-Louise showed herself upon the balcony of the Préfecture where she was staying; then received the authorities, accepted flowers, and held a reception for the men and women of the town. After a second appearance on the balcony she attended at the Comédie, where an act of *La Rosière* was performed, preceded by an appropriate prologue. From the Comédie she was taken to the Mairie, where she was received by the principal ladies of the town, and from which she saw the illuminations. Notwithstanding all these diversions she returned to the Préfecture by nine o'clock.

The following day a page arrived from the Emperor, bringing from Compiègne three pheasants shot by his Imperial and Royal Master. She stopped for lunch at Sillery, with the Senator Comte de Valence; at half-past five she arrived at Vitry-sur-Seine, where she stayed at the Sous-Préfecture and saw no one except Prince Schwarzenberg and Comtesse de Metternich, who had come from Paris to meet her.

This was the final stage : next day would bring her to the ceremonies of the handing over at which the Emperor would be called upon to play a singularly difficult part, since it would involve the *rôles* of father, sovereign, and husband. The Empress left for Soissons. When she reached the Courcelles post-house * it was pouring in torrents, and a short stout man, drenched with rain, was waiting under the church porch. He was accompanied by only one Cavalier with flowing hair, in full uniform. The mysterious man hurried forward to look, but the Equerry had already lowered the step, opened the carriage door and proclaimed, " The Emperor."

The Emperor entered the carriage and embraced *his wife*, who was quite embarrassed by his looks and manners.

No more delay ; no dinner at Soissons, nothing less than post haste, and that was too slow for Napoleon. They hurried past the post-houses and rolled on towards Compiègne, where they arrived at ten o'clock through a deluge that extinguished the lamps and chilled the spectators and guards, who had eaten nothing. The family who assembled at the foot of the staircase, were hurriedly presented, but the little girls with their baskets of flowers and the citizens who had come to offer congratulations, he ignored. In the apartment provided for the Empress he improvised a supper to which Caroline alone was

* Where they change horses.

admitted as a third party. Afterwards he asked:
"What instructions have you received from your
parents?" "To belong entirely to you and to obey
you in all things," replied the bride, so he took her at
her word!

Next day at noon the women of the Empress
served the Emperor's *déjeuner* beside her bed. "Am
I truly married?" he inquired of Cardinal Fesch, to
which the Cardinal, after some hesitation, replied in
the affirmative. So it was all right; besides which
there was the precedent of Henri IV. Nevertheless,
after two hours' acquaintance, the procedure might
have appeared brutal and this wooing unceremonious,
had Marie-Louise not been a Princess of Austria!
Martainville made a song about it, and the denizens
of the Faubourg scrambled for copies, hoping to dis-
concert the Emperor with them. This did not affect
him at all, and among the people there was no dis-
pleasure at his impetuosity!

A crowd was awaiting the Empress at Compiègne.
First the Emperor's family, consisting of the King
and Queen of Holland and the King and Queen of
Westphalia, Princess Pauline and Prince Borghese,
the King and Queen of Naples, the Grand Duke and
Grand Duchess of Baden, the Grand Duke of Würzburg, Prince Schwarzenberg, Count and Countess
Metternich, Comte Clary. The Italian household—
Codronchie, Litta, Caprara, Ferraroli, then the Ministers Bassano, Cadore, Otranto, Daru. Lastly, the
whole of the Emperor's staff.

The Princes and Princesses had received invita-

tions at their own homes from the quartermaster of
the Palace, but as each Princess was allotted accommodation for one lady only and each Prince for one
gentleman, their suites were lodged in the *hôtels* hired
for them, for it was not considered sufficient to present
to the Empress all who were on duty during this
journey, besides the officers and ladies of the Household who had not taken part in it, such as Colonels,
Generals of the Guard, and the Grand Officers of
France and Italy ; but there still remained the
Duchesses and Princesses and the wives of the Grand
Officers. These arrived on the 28th to be presented
on the 29th. The invitation was as follows : " Court
dress must be worn. As there will be great difficulty
in obtaining post horses, particularly for the return,
you should, if possible, bring your own." Twenty-
one leagues ! However, it was a great honour and
eagerly sought after. Three relays were required
which necessitated twelve horses, besides one for the
outrider who preceded the carriage. Court dress was
essential, as it was compulsory for the presentations ;
but Charbonnier, the fashionable coiffeur, had arranged
to be at Compiègne, otherwise the Grand Marshal
would lend his wife's waiting-woman !

After this brief honeymoon, Napoleon wrote to the
Emperor of Austria :

" Monsieur, my brother and father-in-law, your
Majesty's daughter has already been here two
days. She fulfils all my hopes, and these two days I
have not ceased to give and to receive from her the
proofs of the tender sentiments that unite us. We

are in perfect agreement. I shall do everything to promote her happiness and shall owe mine to your Majesty. Your Majesty will therefore permit me to thank you for the splendid present you have made me and your paternal heart may rejoice in the assurance of the welfare of your beloved child."

To which he added : " Your Imperial Majesty must never doubt my sentiments of esteem and high regard nor above all the tenderness I have vowed to her." Was this not indeed a futile effusion, whereof Martainville had betrayed the secret ?

By the Emperor's own direction, they departed for Saint-Cloud on April 2 ; but the religious marriage would be celebrated at the Tuileries. Accordingly, on March 30, at midday, he left Compiègne in a coach with the Empress and the Queen of Naples. On entering the department of Seine-et-Oise, likewise on their entry into the department of the Seine, they received congratulations from the Préfets and the Departmental Authorities. Between Stains and Gagny, at 4.40, the Préfet, accompanied by the Sous-Préfet and fifty-one Mayors, surrounded also by an immense crowd on foot and on horseback, received the Emperor and Empress in front of a marvellously decorated pavilion. "The weather was foggy, cold and damp, but hindered no one," said Madame de Beaumarchais. "There were at least four hundred carriages, and crowds of ladies from Paris, exclusive of young men on prancing horses. It was a counterpart of Longchamp. Their Majesties were very late. . . . Unfortunately the Emperor was in a hurry to arrive at Saint-Cloud, where he was expected at five o'clock, so in military fashion he cut short the speeches; of which he had not heard a syllable. The carriages did not stop for more than five minutes, then the horses were whipped up and the cortège went off at full speed. At Porte Maillot the horses were changed. The Emperor's equipage formed a procession composed of five carriages drawn by six horses and two having eight, escorted by Dragoons and Chasseurs of the Guards.

A salvo of one hundred guns together with the band of the Foot Guards and lines of Grenadiers greeted them at Saint-Cloud. At the foot of the Grand Staircase the Princes, Princesses, and the Grand Dignitaries who had returned from Compiègne waited to salute their Majesties as they passed through the Grand Apartments to those of the Empress. In the evening there was a family dinner, which should have been followed by a presentation of the Italian Court ladies, but this was, however, postponed owing to a change in the programme. "On the day of the Empress's arrival at Saint-Cloud, no presentations will be made, except of the Princes and Princesses of the Imperial Family and of the Grand Dignitaries who will be presented on her Majesty's arrival. Should there be a reception after dinner none but persons who have been presented will be admitted to it."

All these details were of the utmost importance in the mind of the Emperor. A Commission of Exterior relations had been charged to inquire whether the ceremonial arranged at Vienna had been in conformity with that followed on previous occasions, and to ascertain that no possible slight had been shown to the Ambassador Extraordinary. So much for Vienna. In Paris the alterations in the programme of ceremonies were so numerous that it became necessary to suspend the distribution of the sheets already printed on March 23, as they were being revised up to the last hour. Investigations were made as to the witnesses who had assisted at the marriage of Louis XV., and Louis XVI., on either side. Eventually, after a serious examination, Duroc informed the Grand Master there should be no witnesses. The following question was put to d'Hauterive : " What was the position of the Ambassador of the Nation of a foreign Princess, upon the occasion of her marriage with a French Sovereign or Prince in person according to ancient custom ? " After an exhaustive search d'Hauterive excused himself for lack of documentary evidence. The same, however, was not the case with regard to the notifications of the marriage : he was able to avail himself of the constant usage of the Court of France, at least since the reign of Louis XIV., by which the marriages of the Royal Family had been notified by Ambassadors or diplomatic agents, and was therefore able to decide against the *gentilhommes ordinaires* of the King, who, in 1778, had claimed the prerogative of notifying the birth of Princes and Princesses of the Royal Family at foreign courts. As a matter of fact, the Emperor had not yet resuscitated the *gentilhommes ordinaires*. On this occasion, diplomatic agents would suffice ;

later on, for the birth of the Princes, further arrangements could be made.

To return to presentations, the following were made on the day of the civil marriage. First the Ministers, the Cardinals, and the Grand Officers of the Empire or those who had precedence and enjoyed the like prerogatives ; next the wives of Ministers and Grand Officers. No other presentations were to be made, although a large concourse would attend on that day at Saint-Cloud. " It will be permissible to take up a position as His Majesty passes. The curtsies will constitute a presentation, care must therefore be taken that each is according to precedence and that the wives take among themselves the rank of their husbands until after the presentations ; the guests will not be admitted promiscuously."

The decisions as to details of etiquette were innumerable because they would constitute a precedent, and had to include the two Courts of France and Italy and would in future be the model for Naples, Madrid, Amsterdam, Cassel, Florence, and wherever else there were Napoleonic Courts. The Emperor appeared to take a singular pleasure in this meticulous and sometimes childish labour. He delighted in it and elaborated it. Doubtless he saw points in it which fifty years of democracy hinder us from appreciating, and for which a parallel could hardly be found even in the so-called Monarchical States. He fastened on them as if they were serious matters, and if he varied the details, it was because he brought to bear on them such differences of appreciation as usually attach to minutiæ.

A ceremony of a peculiar character preceded the marriage. On March 31, the Comte de Rémusat, First Chamberlain and Master of the Wardrobe, set forth at eleven in the morning from the Tuileries with three Court carriages, preceded and followed by an escort of twenty-five men. He was received at the door of the Archbishop's Palace by two Canons, and at the foot of the staircase by two Vicars General, and was conducted by three Vicars General and six Canons to the chamber in which the crown and mantle of the Empress were deposited. These were carried to his carriage and deposited on the front seat, while he sat respectfully at the back. The first carriage contained four Canons in cassocks and long cloaks ; the second, the crown and mantle, with the Bishop of Liége and the Master of the Wardrobe ; the third, two Vicars General and two Canons. On arrival at the Tuileries, while M. de Rémusat and the Bishop of Liége bore the Imperial mantle into the Emperor's chamber and handed it over to the Grand Chamberlain, the sentries of the Salle des Gardes presented arms and the drums beat a salute. M. de Montesquieu deposited the mantle in the chapel and mounted a military guard over it.

The cortège with its escort continued on its way to Saint-Cloud. On its arrival it received a salute from the sentries of the Salle des Gardes and drummers. The Deputy Governor of the Palace received the cortège at the entrance to the Chapel, in which the crown was deposited upon a cushion in the centre, where it was guarded by two attendants while it remained there. This crown was the subject of a special edict of the Emperor.

"On the day of her marriage," he wrote, "the Empress will wear the coronation crown which is not beautiful but which has a particular significance which I desire to attach to my dynasty. It is only to be worn on the most solemn occasions. For ordinary ceremonies the Empress will wear the closed diamond crown which has no special feature, and which I have ordered to be made for her out of the crown diamonds. On the day after the marriage she will wear the closed diamond crown for her reception."

So anxious was the Emperor that everything should proceed according to his regulations that he wrote on the margin of one of the numerous drafts submitted to him by the Grand Master of the Ceremonies, entitled *Arrangements for the Marriage of His Majesty*, "Returned to the Grand Master of Ceremonies for transmission to each Grand Officer, in order that every precaution shall be taken for the prompt execution of each part in the present arrangements." This he signed.

Zaïre was performed at the Court Theatre on March 31 ; this was Marie-Louise's first introduction to the French theatre. Evidently the choice was made by the Emperor, for no subordinate would have suggested it !

On April 1, in the Gallery of Saint-Cloud, the Civil Marriage was solemnised. A platform had been erected on which were placed two thrones surmounted by a canopy. At the foot of the platform and at one

side of it were an inkstand and the Registers of the
Civil State, arranged on a cloth-covered table. The
Masters and Officials of the Ceremonies had placed the
officers and ladies not on duty behind the platform ;
in front of it all the privileged ladies, Ambassadors,
Cardinals, and Ministers, each of whom held an important office or took a prominent position. At two
o'clock the cortège started, displaying all the pomp of
France and Italy before and behind the Emperor.
Their Majesties seated themselves upon their thrones.
The Princes of the Imperial Family and the Princes
who ranked as Grand Dignitaries sat upon chairs on
either side of them according to their family rank.
The Secretary of the Civil State of the Imperial Family
was in front of the table. The Emperor being seated,
the Grand Master of the Ceremonies proceeded to
announce the Prince Arch-Chancellor, who thereupon
placed himself before the Emperor's throne and after
an obeisance, proclaimed, " In the name of the Emperor " ; whereupon their Majesties rose. He then
continued : " Sire, does your Imperial and Royal
Majesty declare that you will take in matrimony her
Imperial and Royal Highness Marie-Louise Arch-
Duchess of Austria, here present ? " The Emperor
replied in the exact words used by Cambacérès.
After which the question was put to the Arch-Duchess,
who replied, whereupon Cambacérès concluded : " In
the name of the Emperor and of the Law I declare
that His Imperial and Royal Majesty Napoleon,
Emperor of the French, King of Italy, and Her
Imperial and Royal Highness the Arch-Duchess

Marie-Louise are united in matrimony." Their Majesties then resumed their seats. The table was placed before them and the Grand Master of Ceremonies handed them the pen. They remained seated while they signed, the members of the family signed standing, followed by the Arch-Chancellor and Secretary of State. The Grand Master announced the ceremony over, whereupon the cortège re-formed and returned to the apartments of the Empress.

After dinner their Majesties adjourned to the private drawing-room, where the suite, who were to accompany them to the play, had assembled. The procession then passed through the Great Apartments and the illuminated Orangery. *Iphigénie en Aulide* was performed ; truly a peculiar choice !

After the play the Emperor escorted the Empress to her apartment, but on leaving she accompanied him to the first salon, for this was a false exit. It had been arranged at first that he should sleep at Trianon, secondly at the *Pavillon d'Italie* in the park of Saint-Cloud, nevertheless he remained in the apartment of the Empress.

The park was illuminated and the Grand Cascade spouted fire ; Debucourt utilised this subject for one of his finest engravings. Coloured lights played on the fountains, amusements of all kinds were provided under the trees. An immense crowd had assembled, but the wind blew tempestuously, and the rain fell in torrents.

At daybreak the weather was still uncertain, but the sun appeared as the first gun announced their departure for the Tuileries where the religious marriage would be celebrated. After the Empress had been robed, the Emperor joined her, and assisted at the symbolical ceremony, at which the Ladies-in-waiting of France and Italy and the Mistress of the Robes, placed on her head the coronation crown brought from the chapel, by a master of the ceremonies escorted by four ushers. The Empress was wearing the crown diamonds and a superb marriage robe embroidered in jewels and spangles, made by Leroy for 12,000 francs. The Emperor wore a Spanish costume of white satin embroidered in gold, the mantle of which was covered with golden bees. On his head he wore a cap of black velvet ornamented with eight rows of diamonds and three white feathers fastened by a knot, in the middle of which the Regent diamond blazed. The cap did not fit, it had to be altered twenty times, every possible way of wearing it had been attempted, but finally it was pronounced satisfactory.

The following was the order of the procession when the carriages were marshalled : Lancers of the Guard, Chasseurs of the Guard, Dragoons of the Guard, with their bands and standards. Then thirty-six carriages of six horses for the Masters of Ceremonies, the Chamberlains of France and Italy, *Les Grands Aigles* of the Empire, the Ministers, the Ladies of the Court of France and Italy, the Grand Officers of Italy, the Grand Officers of France, the Prince Grand Dignitaries, the Princes and Princesses of the family. The empty carriage of the Empress drawn by eight horses,

E

between the chief Equerries of Italy and her First Equerry, behind which rode the aides-de-camp. After this the coronation carriage appeared conveying their Majesties at a walking pace drawn by bay horses, laden with pages and flanked by Colonels-General of the Guard. Various other carriages followed, after which mounted Grenadiers completed the cortège.

From Porte Maillot to the Tuileries the route was lined with troops ; at one o'clock a salvo announced the arrival of the cortège at the Arc de Triomphe, which looked magnificent erected in canvas and wood according to the plan of Chalgren and ornamented with bas-reliefs painted by Lafitte. The Préfet of the Seine delivered an address and led the authorities of the city who followed on foot. In the Champs Elysées, bands were posted at given distances. Young girls of the Faubourg offered flowers. At the Pont Tournant, a triumphal arch painted with decorations had been prepared for a grand orchestra beneath which the carriages passed. The people of the cortège alighted in the vestibule of the Tuileries and grouped themselves on the grand staircase or waited in the salons allotted to them.

The Emperor retired to his room while the Court dress of the Empress was being changed for the Imperial mantle, after which the procession reformed and moved forward by way of the Galerie du Bord de l'Eau divided into nine aisles of varying size by arches supported by columns of precious marbles, in the presence of eight thousand guests, four thousand

men and four thousand women. With great discretion and taste, the ladies had been grouped in such
a way that their dresses, seen through the whole
length of the arches to the end of the gallery, afforded
a truly dazzling spectacle. The guests had arrived
at seven in the morning ; it was now three in the
afternoon.

From this gallery the Emperor and Empress
passed along to the great *Salon Carré*, which appeared
more like a magnificent ballroom hung with silken
draperies than a chapel, save for the altar. Four
hundred persons occupied the galleries round the hall.
In front of the altar, which was entirely silver gilt,
were placed two seats and a Prie-Dieu surmounted by
a canopy. Seats were provided for the Bishops,
Cardinals, Senators, State Councillors, and Members
of the Legislative Body. The gallery was opened at
three o'clock. Cardinal Fesch advanced to the door
of the chapel to receive their Majesties and gave
them Holy Water. From the moment he entered, the
Emperor scrutinised everything, and observed a
shortage of Cardinals. His wrath with those who had
absented themselves can best be understood from his
letter to Eugène concerning the Cardinal-Archbishop
of Bologna. "You will inform him of my great
indignation at the infamous conduct of one on whom
I have heaped benefits, and have made Cardinal-
Archbishop and Senator, whom I have protected and
whose notorious debaucherie I have cloaked by the
intervention of my authority, thereby interrupting
the course of criminal justice at Bologna." The

Emperor observed and summed up everything in a glance, as this letter shows, written to the Minister of Public Worship, Bigot de Paéameneu, in which he forbade them to wear the insignia of their office. " It is because we consider them already suspended, that we refuse to allow them to wear the ecclesiastical distinctions and costume of Cardinals."

He grew calmer, however, and the Mass proceeded with appropriate solemnity. After the Gospel, the Premier Bishop produced the Testament for their Majesties to kiss, and waved the censer before them. At the Offertorium the King of Holland bore the Regalia of the Emperor, and the Queen of Naples that of the Empress, who was accompanied by her Lady-in-waiting and Mistress of the Robes. A host of Bishops were employed in the various parts of the ceremony. The *Te Deum* followed the Mass, after which they returned through the large gallery. When the Emperor had left, the crowd began to congregate and the gallery was thronged as on the days the Museum opened. Suddenly at the doors of the chapel an usher proclaimed, " The Emperor ! " whereupon, as if electrified, every one jumped over the balustrade, finding a place where he could. Instantly a way was cleared and the procession moved on as majestically as before.

It halted in the Galerie de Diane ; the Emperor, with the Empress and the family, retired to his salon. In her bed-chamber the Empress was relieved of the mantle and the crown, which were given back to the Grand Chamberlain, to be returned to Notre

Dame with the same ceremonies as on the previous evening. Their Majesties showed themselves on the balcony of the Salle des Maréchaux and witnessed the march past of the Corps de la Garde, which acclaimed the Sovereigns by presenting arms.

It must not be supposed that this concluded the proceedings. The *fêtes* were so organised that there was not a moment for dinner. Regnaud de Saint Jean d'Angely provided a very *récherché* cold dinner in the Salle de la Section de l'Intérieur. The Corps Diplomatique roamed about the Palace in search of a meal. M. Regnaud invited the Ambassador of Austria. The dinner was very gay, very animated. Great fun was made of the Russians who could not find places. M. de Metternich, happy and elated, talked and cracked jokes. A crowd had collected beneath the windows. M. de Metternich went on to the balcony with a glass of champagne in his hand, exclaiming : " To the health of the King of Rome." " We are not yet good enough courtiers," remarked Regnaud to M. de Barante.

At seven o'clock, however, in the Salle de Spectacle of the Tuileries (the stage having been replaced by a decoration similar to the one at the other end of the hall), the Imperial banquet was served. The Emperor dined with his family, of whom only Joseph and Lucien were absent, seated upon a platform surmounted by a canopy. Members of the Court were arranged in front of them in the orchestra and boxes. The Civic Dignitaries occupied the second tier of boxes and the apartments through which their

Majesties passed on their way to the banquet. By six o'clock the Masters of Ceremonies had marshalled the guests in the Salon de la Paix. The Grand Maréchal having announced everything ready, the cortège passed through the Grand Apartments to the banqueting hall. Grace was said by the Grand Almoners, and the band, which was placed in the top tier of boxes, discoursed topical music. Nothing could be more magnificent or more formal.

The cortège returned to the Salle des Maréchaux where their Majesties reappeared on the balcony. Afterwards a cantata by Arnault, set to Méhul's music, was given by the chorus from Gluck's *Iphigénie*. Every kind of music was heard outside the Palace. A rocket sent up from the Palace gave the signal for a display of fireworks over the whole of the Champs Elysées, after which the cortège retired to the apartment of the Empress. At a signal from the Emperor the dignitaries retired, then the princes and princesses. The Empress entered her boudoir. The Emperor went up to his own apartment to prepare for the night. Considering how many hours the Empress had been standing, she must have felt satiated with ceremonies, even had she liked them. It was thought, however, she might like to inspect the wedding presents which had been placed in her private apartment. Possibly she might have preferred the fireworks! The Grande Allée of the Tuileries was one blaze of light, hung with thousands of coloured lights. Thirteen triumphal arches were similarly illuminated. The decorations in the flower garden were less elaborate, but the approach to the Pont Tournant, the chestnut avenues, and the terraces were lit up with hanging lanterns. The Temple of Glory was outlined as it would appear when completed. The Temple of Hymen was simulated on the towers of Notre Dame, and on the Pantheon flared an antique tripod.

At two o'clock in the Champs Elysées, the most marvellous variety of entertainments began. At the Carré des Jeux there were five theatres : wrestlers of Herculean strength, dancers on the tight-rope, M. Olivier's spectacle, the Theatre of Picturesque and Mechanical Views, the Theatre of Intangible Shadows, two roundabouts, two switchbacks, two see-saws, one Egyptian bird, two greasy poles, two games of the dragon, six bands to dance to, an orchestral concert with 120 musicians, troops of singers engaged to sing the *Chansons du Gouvernement*, a troop of Savoyards with their bagpipes ; besides these Madame Furioso on the tight-rope with itinerant musicians and a brass band. At the Carré Marigny, the same wrestlers, tight-rope dancers, entertainments by M. Préjean, M. Lauranzo Frederici and Séraphin, besides Pyrrhic fires and Chinese shadows. At the Carré de la Pompe (chez Ledoyon), at the Carré de la Laiterie, they were as numerous, but at the Carré de l'Elysée bands for quadrilles and roundabouts predominated. Among all this variety something new might be found here to interest each stranger.

Of all these fleeting wonders, what has survived ? In front of the façade of the Corps Législatif we may see the six statues that were unveiled on the occasion of the Emperor's marriage ; those of d'Aguesseau, Colbert, l'Hôpital, Sully, and last but not least Themis and Minerva, which latter amid the adornments of modern Paris alone recalls the past.

Next day, April 3, at ten o'clock in the morning, the Mounted Heralds distributed the Marriage Medals (similar in size to the Coronation Medals) among the populace, 20,000 of which were silver, 500 gold. At the Coronation there had been four sizes : 1390 in gold, 74,450 in silver ; the distribution had dwindled.

Official France was presented to the Emperor by the Grand Chamberlain and to the Empress by her Lady-in-waiting. This presentation comprised Ministers, Cardinals, Grand Officers of the Empire, Grands Aigles, Court of the Audit Office, Council of the University, Officers of the Household of the Princes and Princesses, Generals of Divisions, Court of Appeal, Archbishops, Préfets, Clergy of Paris, Court of Criminal Justice, Brigadier-Generals, Bishops, Authorities of Paris, City Mayors, in fact thousands of individuals came to pay homage, insomuch that Marie-Louise wrote thus to her father : " Yesterday more than 1500 people were presented to me. I felt so ill all the time, owing to the diamond crown which was so heavy I could hardly bear it ; consequently I saw absolutely no one."

Such was to be her lot !

CHAPTER IV

AFTER devoting three days to Paris and Saint-Cloud, the Emperor set off again to Compiègne, where he held audiences, received congratulations and oaths of fidelity. Excursions, plays, hunting parties, concerts, receptions, and all kinds of functions took place. "Although the receptions held in Paris were reckoned as representations, nevertheless, after Sunday, fifteen men with the same number of women were daily to be presented to the Empress, from among those who had already been received, as well as those who had not yet been presented. During the twenty-four hours of their visit to Compiègne these persons would be duly accredited and would enjoy all prerogatives." Accordingly, thirty a day of these new people were to be received by the Empress in her gallery as she passed through to attend the play.

The plays were usually performed by the Comédie Française, e.g. Le Cid, Phèdre, Andromaque, Britannicus, Le Misanthrope, Tartufe, also La Gageure, Imprévue, La Jeunesse de Henri V., Le Secret du Ménage, Les Projets de Mariage. The selection of Britannicus appears injudicious, for how could so clever a man as the husband of Madame de Rémusat have chosen a play entirely concerned with divorce, having a dialogue full of the grossest innuendoes ?

At length this journey came to an end, having necessitated the presence of sixty-seven persons, besides fifteen ladies in the suite of the Queens and Princesses, to whom, by a decree of April 19, the Emperor had granted *prérogatives du voyage ;* besides all those who came from Paris to be presented or do homage.

The Emperor passed his days and nights with the Empress. Even the most urgent business could hardly separate him from her for a few moments. He would convene a Council and arrive two hours after it had assembled. He almost suppressed private audiences. Every one, except Marie-Louise, wondered if this mode of living could continue. He treated her to his favourite habit of slapping ! He would pinch her neck or her cheeks ; if she showed annoyance he took her in his arms, embraced her and called her *grosse bête*, on which term of endearment they made peace ! Marie-Louise, however, thought his manners a little vulgar.

At the close of the visit to Compiègne on April 26, their Majesties set out for Belgium. They were accompanied by a numerous suite which was divided into three parties—one started twelve hours before their Majesties, one accompanied them, and one followed later. Seeing that the first comprised twelve coaches, seventy-two carriage horses and four hacks, the second ten coaches, sixty-two carriage horses, and ten hacks, and the third eleven coaches, sixty-five carriage horses and four hacks, we may picture the commotion caused by such a procession, and the general dislocation of traffic which must have resulted.

The military escort consisted of 200 mounted Chasseurs, 200 Polish Light Horse, 80 mounted Grenadiers, 30 picked Gendarmes, 140 Marines of the Guard. Duroc arranged everything beforehand, even to the itinerary and the various stopping-places. We shall see that the accommodation was frequently indifferent, causing the Empress to complain, but nothing better was available. The impression France made upon Marie-Louise in this first journey is of fundamental importance. The Empress apparently was inclined to ridicule and could criticise people, at any rate those whom she disliked. Those she liked were very few, consequently with the exception of the Duchesse de Montebello scarcely any one escaped her criticisms. But here is her own account of the journey.

"I set out from Compiègne, delighted with the idea of such a pleasant journey. I had never before travelled without sadness, but now felt the undertaking would be delightful and am certain I shall love travelling to distraction. The Queen of Naples and the Grand Duke of Wurtzburg accompanied us. It was a particular pleasure to have the latter with me, he is so kind and vivacious.

"We left Compiègne on April 27 at nine in the morning. The country as far as St. Quentin is very pretty, even beautiful, also very fertile. All along the road are little hills covered with fruit trees now in full bloom, and fields of the most fascinating green intersected by small streams bordered with willows. There are many hamlets and villages, but what struck me most was the quantity of wind-mills.

" In every place the Emperor was received by the inhabitants with ringing of bells and firing of salutes, expressions of a devotion as simple as it was touching. Everywhere the young ladies presented us with flowers and poems, most of the latter were very poor.

" We arrived at St. Quentin at midday and were lodged in the Préfecture where everything was uncomfortable and dirty, and what was worse was the fact that I was a quarter of a league away from the Emperor. He took luncheon at once and rode off to visit the fortifications and the source of the St. Quentin canal, which had just been finished from a plan provided by the Emperor himself. I went to bed with lumbago, not yet being accustomed to continuous travelling over paved roads.

" The Emperor made me get up at four o'clock to visit a cotton-mill belonging to the prefect, which is remarkable, the machines are wonderful inventions.

" On our return we received the chief officials. The Emperor conversed with them for over two hours. These audiences are enough to kill one, for it is necessary to stand all the time! Afterwards young ladies presented me with specimens from their factories.

" The Emperor was much amused while telling me of an accident which happened to M. Joan,* who,

---

* The Empress writes *Joan*. She refers to Jouan, knight of the Legion of Honour, March 8, 1807, surgeon-major attached to the Ambulance of the Imperial Household in the Grand Armée. He was in all the campaigns.—F. M.

while galloping without looking where he was going, was caught on the branch of a tree ; the horse went on and after a few minutes he fell to the ground without hurting himself in the least. Malicious tongues say that for more than an hour he thought himself dead, which is very like him !

" After dinner there was a ball at the town hall and a cantata was sung which contained the most fulsome compliments. The Queen opened the ball by dancing a *Contredance française* with Chamberlain de Metternich.

" The town of St. Quentin has about 12,000 inhabitants. It is very old and badly built, but commercially flourishing. The local manufactures are longcloth, linen, cambric, leather, and morocco ; the trade in cotton brings in over 3 millions annually.

" Next day we left St. Quentin at seven in the morning, and after passing through the whole of the city, which is not very large, we arrived at the canal, where we found two gondolas awaiting us. The canal begins at St. Quentin and terminates at Cambrai, where it joins the Scheldt. It is over 22 leagues in length having 23 locks, and is very wide and deep. We went on board and continued our way beneath a blazing sun which gave us terrible headaches. We reached the first tunnel into which the water had not yet been admitted and entered carriages in order to pass through it. The length is a quarter of a league, entirely cut out of the rock. The vault is very high and was illuminated by two rows of lamps which made a magnificent effect. It is a masterpiece, unique of its kind. We continued our journey by carriage as far as the entrance to the second tunnel, where tents

had been pitched for lunch, which we welcomed like
famished travellers. We went through this tunnel,
which is a league and a half long, in a boat rowed by
men, which was not very serviceable, for it let in two
inches of water, which wetted our feet, but as there
was no means of remedying it, one had to bear up
gaily, which for me was not difficult as I have an iron
constitution which nothing injures. In addition we
narrowly escaped capsizing because the fat Prince
Schwarzenberg was continually leaning out of the
boat and his weight threw it all on one side. This
second tunnel was illuminated like the first, and at the
end of every hundred *toises* (about 650 feet) there was
a shaft to let in daylight. After an hour and a half
we reached the mouth of the canal and got into the
carriages again.

" We saw the source of the Scheldt, that majestic
river, which 40 leagues farther on is so wide and deep
that the largest battleships can navigate it, but is
here so narrow that one can easily cross it by a
standing jump. It passes twice under the canal,
which is carried over it by means of an aqueduct ;
the bridge is so narrow that we were obliged to leave
the carriages which were then lifted over by men.
This affair delayed us more than an hour and put the
Queen of Naples into such a bad temper that no one
could speak to her for the rest of the day. I cannot
understand how people when travelling can grumble
and get impatient over such trifling accidents ! To
me they were very insignificant in comparison with
all I had had to put up with in other journeys, of
which I had never complained.

" We went on board again half a league from

Cambrai, and at half-past three entered the basin at the end of the canal, where a number of trading vessels, laden with coal, were waiting to enter the canal to carry their cargoes to Paris.

" On reaching the Hôtel de Ville I went to bed, for the sun had given me a shocking headache. I was, however, quite pleased with myself at not having grumbled once during the journey. Truly the bad temper of several of the ladies was enough to prevent me from fault finding.

" Cambrai is a very ancient city and indeed was once a Roman Colony. In 1520 a Treaty of Peace was concluded in this place, when two princesses conducted the greater part of the negotiations, hence it became known as the Ladies' Treaty. Xinrlo (*sic*) (Fénelon) is buried in this town, and I felt very indignant to notice that he, who so well deserved a fine mausoleum erected out of gratitude by his diocesans, was interred in a wooden coffin ; while others, whose chief merit was the fact that they were wealthy enough to found churches, had magnificent monuments.

" Cambrai has 30,000 to 40,000 inhabitants and manufactures the same articles of commerce as St. Quentin. There are also many soap factories.

" I got up at seven o'clock to see the procession of waggons in the square, on which, amid a vast concourse of people, sat some 200 young girls dressed in white, who are clothed and fed by the ladies of the town.

" After dinner, which was at eight o'clock, we received the local authorities and the young ladies who brought me cambric and lace. At ten o'clock

there was a superb display of fireworks, after which
the ladies and the young girls of Cambrai were
presented to me.

"I know nothing more embarrassing for any one
so timid and awkward as myself than to receive daily
some sixty ladies who are absolute strangers to me,
but with whom, nevertheless, I am obliged to converse.
An attack of vertigo relieved me this time from a
situation in which I usually say many foolish things.

"The Queen of Naples left us here and with her
Chr. de Metternich, so much the better. I do not
regret them, but it was very ungallant of the Grand
Duke of Wiszburg (Wurtzbourg) to desert us to
follow the Queen of Naples. It is only too true that
when love and friendship are in the balance, poor
tranquil friendship has to go to the wall!

"On the 29th the Bishop said Mass for us at
eight o'clock, and we left at nine. The country
round Cambray and for some leagues beyond it, is
flat and not as fine as that from Compiègne to Saint-
Quentin.

"We passed through Bouchain, a small fortified
town built by Pepin the Short, in memory of his
victory over Thierry King of the Goths. Denain is
three leagues farther on, where the Maréchal de
Villars gained a victory over the troops of Prince
Eugène. Louis XIV. erected an obelisk inscribed
with two verses of the *Henriade* to commemorate this
event.

"We reached Valenciennes at eleven o'clock, a
pretty little town with 20,000 inhabitants. It is
situated in a very pleasant valley, and its fortifications,
which are still in excellent preservation, were con-

structed by Vauban. The city is rather dirty, but does a flourishing trade in a kind of lace which is much in request and gives occupation to many women in the neighbourhood of the town. Here the Duchesse de Montebello passed her girlhood. She said it pleased her to see again the places in which she had spent the happiest period of her life; but was much annoyed at being invited to lunch by the Emperor, for it prevented her visiting her grandmother whom she had not seen for fifteen years.

" After lunch the Emperor received the authorities and I the young ladies, who brought me lace.

" We stopped a short time at Mons to see the beginning of a canal which is to serve between that town and Paris. There was at one time a Chapter of Canonesses here. There is much coal-mining on the outskirts of this town, and the dust on the main road is so black that one's complexion becomes like that of a chimney-sweep.

" After an hour's journey the country from Mons to Brussels becomes very flat, resembling a beautiful English park, and continually increases in beauty and variety as one approaches Brussels, which is situated in a delightful valley watered by the Senne. The valleys around are bordered by low hills clothed with forests or fruit trees.

" It was evening when we reached Brussels. It appeared to be an exceedingly fine town, but I could not judge of it very well for we passed through it hurriedly. The scenery is still more beautiful between Brussels and Laeken. The Brussels canal lies between avenues of magnificent trees behind which are country houses with charming gardens.

F

"At the end of an hour we climbed a steep hill and arrived at Laeken, which is rather a handsome palace bought by the Emperor from the Duke of Saxe-Teschen.

"On our arrival the Emperor went at once to see the castle. There are two very fine suites of apartments on the ground floor, which is raised by a dozen steps above the garden. There are also a number of rooms between the ground floor and the first story and on the first floor itself.

"My first consideration was to take a bath to rid myself of the horrible black dust. I do not know if the bath upset me because I got into it while still very hot, but I was seized with frightful cramp in the stomach, with colic. The Emperor must needs send for Monsieur Jouan, who, after many florid and pompous phrases, informed the Emperor that I was going to have a child and should have a miscarriage if I continued my journey. The Emperor believed him, which annoyed me so much that I suffered still more.

"To revenge myself on M. Jouan I pretended to be very ill. He hurried in, felt my pulse, which he declared he could not find, so rubbed my nose with vinegar. After five minutes I pretended to return to consciousness, for he was by this time talking of bleeding me. This little incident left me with a very strange opinion of him, for only ignorance or the wiles of a clever courtier could have made him act as he did. I prefer to think it was the former. I should despise him too much if it were the latter. It is, however, true that we are living in such charming surroundings that I must accustom myself to them. I fear, nevertheless, that this will be difficult !

" The next day, 30th, the Emperor, instead of letting me rest, awakened me at seven in the morning to see the garden. Fortunately, in his sleep he had forgotten M. Jouan's portentous phrases, so there was no further question of leaving me at Brussels.

" The garden is tolerably large and charming, it is planted in the English fashion, there are several buildings and some well-arranged vistas. After lunch, as soon as the Emperor had received the deputations, we set off across the garden, at the end of which is the canal on which we were to embark.

" Here we were rejoined by the Viceroy and the King and Queen of Westphalia, who had arrived from Paris to accompany us on the journey.

" Nothing more beautiful can be imagined than the banks of this canal, and now was the right moment to see it, as all the fruit trees were in blossom. There are many country houses along the left bank.

" The villages are quite Dutch. No French is spoken, and the dialect of the country is a corrupt German called ' Platt-deutsch.' At a quarter of a league from the castle of Schönenberg, one arm of the Senne passes under the canal to rejoin the other, from which it had been separated ; the construction, by means of which this passage is effected without danger to the canal itself, is called *les trois trous*. It is said to be an admirable piece of work.

" We went through four locks, at each of which we were delayed at least five and twenty minutes. There is really nothing more tiresome than a canal voyage. It takes over an hour to travel one league !

" Near Vilvorde is the House of Correction, an immense building intended to accommodate the beggars from the large towns. Such an institution might well be established in every country of Europe.

" Before entering the lock which is close to Malines (Mechlin), the high road crosses the canal by a bridge. Malines (Mechlin) on the left bank of the canal is quite a handsome city. The Cathedral is very fine and has a spire three hundred and forty-eight feet high. There are a good many industries in this town, of which the most important are tanning and hat-making ; but Mechlin is most famous for its lace, which is in great demand and made in various qualities.

" The Archbishop was at the door of the Cathedral with his clergy. I think he is rather like Tartufe !

" Here we began to see many trading vessels large enough to undertake a voyage to the Indies.

" Never have I been so much entertained as during this day, when everything was a novelty to me. I had never seen any ships, so it was impossible to make either the Queen of Westphalia or myself take any part in the conversation. We could already hear the dull boom of the cannon from afar, not unlike the noise of thunder, and saw in the distance a great many masts which were still so far off they appeared like steeple spires.

" Finally, at four o'clock, two hours after the turn of the tide, we entered the Rupel. A lock closes the entrance to it. On the wharf we found Admiral Missiessy, the Minister of Marine, and all the other chief officers, who conducted us by a detestable road to a pretty little gondola in which we embarked upon the Rupel, which flows into the Scheldt, a league farther on, where we saw about 25 gunboats which

are made smaller than a sloop of war. They were
not in commission on account of the ice, which had
been very thick this year.

"After an hour we entered the Scheldt, which is
very broad at this spot. The weather was magnificent.
The sun was setting and there was a dead calm, but I
would gladly have exchanged it for a storm, which I
long to experience. Round a bend in the river, we
saw the fine spectacle of seven battleships which were
not all in commission.

"Really there is nothing so grand as one of these
vessels! A man-of-war is 48 ft. wide, 23 ft. high
above the water and 19 ft. below. Some have 60 to
120 guns. The masts are taller than a three-storied
house and carry a quantity of sails and rigging. A
small gangway leads down to the captain's room, the
council-chamber, and several other quite pretty
cabins. Still farther down one comes to the place
where the sailors sleep, where also the guns are
carried. The hospital and galleys for provisions and
munitions are below the water-level. Lower still
one comes to the magazine in which the powder is
kept.

"When the vessel is in commission there are
sometimes as many as 500 sailors, some of them
being right up the mast head.

"We were saluted by a thousand guns, the report
of which half deafened us, myself in particular, for
since the occasion on which my father made me fire
off an over-loaded cannon, any loud noise now makes
my ear bleed.

"We climbed on board the *Charlemagne,* but it
required courage to accomplish this. The gangway

was like a ladder with the steps so far apart that we had to clamber up on our knees. There was wind enough, moreover, to cause very embarrassing accidents. I am certain we exhibited our legs to the gentlemen, and I vowed never to climb on to a battle-ship again without putting on trousers! The Minister of Marine might really have been gallant enough to have had a better stairway constructed for us, but one sees in everything that he is but a rough sailor. We were saluted by cheers repeated three times.

" One needs to be very agile in boarding a battle-ship for the first time, to avoid laming oneself. I know I returned to Antwerp with a sprain, two lumps on my head, and a gown covered with tar.

" The Scheldt here is half a league wide. I had been told a great deal about the disagreeable move-ment I should experience, but to me when the weather is calm there is no difference between the sea and a river.

" Both banks of the Scheldt are lovely, there are many country houses and charming gardens. The setting sun added to the beauty of the landscape.

" On rounding a little point we came upon Antwerp. Several frigates, four men-of-war, and a vast number of gunboats were lying in the harbour of this fine city.

" The last rays of the sun were gilding the spires of the city and produced a marvellous effect over the Scheldt.

" We disembarked at seven o'clock in the midst of an immense crowd and continued our journey in a carriage to the house of the Préfet, where we were indifferently lodged.

" My room looked on one side upon a little garden, on another upon the court, and on the third upon a little narrow and dark street from which rose such terrible exhalations that I was not able to open the windows during the whole of my stay. We dined and then went to bed.

" On the 1st of May the weather was magnificent. The Emperor went out at break of day to see the fortifications and arranged to meet us for breakfast at the Préfecture Maritime, which is a very fine house. The Emperor made us go there at eight o'clock ; at one he had not arrived. What tedium and impatience we felt while waiting for him may readily be imagined !

" At last we embarked at two o'clock to go on board the *Anversois*. Happily this time the gangway was a little better.

" The Emperor drilled the crew, and dismantled (*fit démonter*) the ship, while the King of Westphalia amused himself by climbing up all the masts. The Emperor also put a Dutch frigate under sail ; after that he went on board the *Dalmate* and the frigate, but I had too vivid a recollection of my two bruises of the previous evening to have any desire to accompany him, so I waited for him on the *Anversois*. As on the previous evening, we were saluted by a thousand cannon. We passed in front of the *Pulstuck*, but as she was not in commission, the Emperor did not board her.

" On returning home I found two rooms on fire. They say this is a sign of good luck. I could have done very well without this sign, for we had a terrible smoke all day. In the evening the Emperor received the authorities and ladies of the town, and on the following day inspected the rest of the fortifications, returning for lunch.

" I was again annoyed with that tiresome M. Jouan, who urged the Emperor not to take me to the Island of Walcheren, also with the Emperor for listening to him. Doctors are real ignoramuses, they do not know that far more harm is done to their patients, even when they are ill, by thwarting them than by letting them do as they wish ; but I can be obstinate when I want anything, and we shall see which of us will prevail !

" The Emperor took me to the dockyard to see the *Friedland* of 84 launched. The dock is where the ships are built. In that of Antwerp several ships and frigates can be constructed at the same time. Their hulls are placed in wooden scaffoldings in which they stay until they are quite complete. There were nine here at this time. It takes nearly a year to construct a vessel, and usually costs two millions.

" When we had reached an amphitheatre that had been prepared expressly for the ceremony, the Archbishop of Malines advanced to bless the ship, all the scaffolding having been removed. At a given signal the last ropes were cut, and I was so terrified lest some one should be crushed that I hurriedly shut my eyes just at the moment when it shot into the water. I heard nothing but a violent noise. They told me the spectacle was magnificent; I pity the people who were obliged to sustain this shock, by which the Scheldt became very much stirred up.

" The Emperor made another tour in the district and I took a drive with the Queen of Westphalia upon the ramparts and about the town. They say that in another year Antwerp will be one of the strongest places of the Empire. There are some tolerably fine streets in the town, which contains 60,000 inhabitants, also some fine mansions, and the churches are said to be very beautiful, but I did not go over any of them.

" The Parish Church contains the tomb of Rubens, and a historical picture in which he painted himself with his father and his wives.

" The tower of the Cathedral is as high and as beautiful as that of Strasbourg. The view from it is said to be superb. I should very much have liked to climb it, but when travelling with the Emperor it is very difficult to amuse and instruct oneself, as it is impossible to do as one likes.

" The Town Hall is a splendid edifice. The dock-yard, where the timber for shipbuilding is kept, is immense. The two docks are magnificent. The Emperor had one of these constructed. The largest can berth forty-two ships of the line. It has just been finished except for two locks which have still to be constructed at the farther end to the Scheldt. These locks are designed to admit vessels into two small adjacent harbours, where they will be sheathed with copper, after they are berthed in the dry dock by opening the sluices at low tide.

" The other dock is upon the river; it will give anchorage to fourteen ships of the line and com-municates with the first dock by a very large lock.

" When peace is made with England, Antwerp will be one of the richest and most important com-mercial towns of the Empire. In the meantime it has already a considerable trade. There are many very wealthy merchants, some of whom have magnificent collections of pictures. Mr. Van Haveren possesses, among others, the famous *Chapeau de Paille* of Rubens.

" There are many charming country houses round Antwerp, but I should dislike to live in this town owing to the unhealthy climate. The neighbourhood is very marshy and nasty smells come from the Scheldt, consequently three-quarters of the inhabitants have fever every year.

" On the 3rd the Emperor went to visit the arsenal, the docks, and the magazines, but I stayed at home to be wearied by my ladies. I am much too undisciplined to spend a whole day in their company, and am only happy with the Duchesse de Montebello, who is natural and good, whereas the others are ill-natured and pretentious.

" In the evening we saw all the ladies of the town.

" On the 4th, the Emperor went again to inspect a ship. I remained at home as my foot hurt me too much to walk. In the evening there was a ball, but being lame I had a good reason for not dancing. Besides, my doctors are so obliging, they provide me with an excuse whenever I want one !

" It was very stormy all day, and hopes of being able to start on the next were given up as the wind was contrary, and as we should have to cross an arm of the sea in order to reach Flushing, we were compelled to wait with patience.

" On the 5th, the weather was still very bad and the storm violent. The Emperor, who was tired of waiting, suddenly decided in the evening to go by

land and start the next morning at five o'clock with as
few people as possible, just clothes for two days and
two sets of attendants.

"It was decided that only the King and Queen of
Westphalia, the Viceroy, the Prince de Neuchâtel,
the Grand Maréchal Duc d'Istrie, the Duchesse de
Montebello, MM. de Beauharnais, de St. Aignan,
de Bondy, and de Montaran, should accompany us,
while the rest were to wait for us at Antwerp.
Accordingly, we left Antwerp on the 6th, three hours
later than the Emperor had arranged (for with him
that always happens).

"The beginning of the journey for a league or so
was quite pleasant, as we passed by a number of
country seats, but at the end of an hour all the beauty
had disappeared, and we found ourselves in a desert
of sand, where there was not a blade of grass, and
where one saw here and there a few stunted fir trees,
of which the largest were no bigger than the smallest
in a certain black forest that I came to know afterwards ! This district formerly belonged to Holland.

"It was only after an interval of two or three
hours that we came upon a little village, these villages
are really charming. I think they are rather like the
description of the oases in the great desert. Dutch
farmers are noted for their extreme cleanliness, which
extends even to their houses, which are very large
and have great square paving-tiles ; most of the houses
are built of brick. They are enclosed with fences
and trees are planted in front of them. Each has
its vegetable garden and orchard, and magnificent
cows graze in the meadows. I have never seen such
fine cattle as in Holland. They are unlike other cows

on account of their size and colouring, which is white with black or brown spots.

"The road became worse every moment. The sand was so deep that it was necessary to harness 12 or 16 horses to each carriage, notwithstanding that we only went at a walking pace !

"The horses are so badly harnessed in this country that it is impossible to hurry them ; instead of bits, cords are put in their mouths, and the traces are so thin that they come to pieces every moment. As the horses of the peasants are requisitioned, each man wants to drive his own steed, there are therefore sometimes as many postilions as horses. I have counted at least a dozen. If we wish to go faster they bewail the hard fate of their animals, and if pressure is brought to bear in order to hurry them, they unyoke the horses and take them away, leaving one stranded in the middle of the sands. This happened to several carriages in our retinue.

"The hour for lunch had long passed ; it was nearly two o'clock, and the Emperor would never allow me to eat in a carriage. He had a fine reason for this, which was that a woman ought never to want to eat. These precious arguments added to the pangs of hunger made me so angry that I had a terrible headache, consequently when we arrived at Breda at four o'clock, I thought I should be obliged to stay there ; however, the Emperor, who treated us like grenadiers, forced us to continue our journey after his lunch !

"We took our meal in a wretched château which formerly belonged to the Prince of Orange.

"Breda is a small and rather pretty town of from 7000 to 8000 inhabitants with excellent fortifications.

" After the Emperor had received the local officials we resumed our journey. I was in such a bad temper that the Emperor was displeased, but feeling quite indifferent I let him scold as much as he liked without answering him.

" There is nothing which quiets men so soon as this method. They are insufferable beings, and should I ever come back in another world, I would certainly not make a second marriage !

" The road was still very monotonous and the weather dreadful. The wind blew horribly, and the rain was so heavy that we were inundated. The Emperor, however, contrary to his usual practice, found the atmosphere stifling, so opened all the windows for the pleasure of opposing my wishes.

" At eight o'clock the Maréchal Duc de Reggio with several generals came to our carriage and assured us that we were only an hour's journey from Bois-le-Duc. However, we did not arrive there until midnight.

" Fortunately my waiting-maid was there, for I felt so ill and fatigued that I went to bed directly without eating. I had dreadful pains in the stomach with fever ; added to this, there was so much noise in the courtyard that it was impossible to sleep. Having sent for M. Bourdier, the consoling news was brought me that he had been left behind at Breda !

" Finally, at one o'clock, I heard my door open (for it had neither bolt nor key), and some one enter the room very softly. It was the Prince de Neu-châtel, who (imagining himself in the Emperor's room) on seeing me was very embarrassed.

" At last, at two o'clock, M. Jouan arrived, half

dead, and covered from head to foot with clay, for he had fallen into a hole. I begged him to give me some antipyrin hetera.* He went to fetch the little medicine chest, but finding all the bottles broken, I had to resign myself, and wait until I should recover without medicine.

" At three o'clock the Duchesse de Montebello arrived ; her carriage had stuck for four hours in the sand in spite of all the efforts of M. de St. Aignan and Prince Aldobrandini. When these gentlemen saw that they could not extricate the carriage, they unyoked the horses, and using a bag of oats for a saddle, went to seek help at Bois-le-Duc, while M. de Beauharnais, instead of assisting them, remained in the carriage grumbling because he could not get on. The Duc de Bassano lost patience because his coachman would not proceed, and got out of his carriage, prepared to chastise the poor wretch severely, but Heaven punished him, for he fell into a pool up to his neck ; although in this predicament he became very polite, the peasant would not pull him out ; he was therefore obliged to remain there until another carriage came to the rescue.

" There was, indeed, a great deal to laugh at next day when the company related their adventures ; but even more amusing experience was in store for the Duchess de Montebello.

" I was so fatigued on the 7th that I did not get out of bed till dinner-time ; moreover, the town and its suburbs were not sufficiently interesting to tempt me to visit them.

" The Emperor went out to inspect the fortifica-

* A febrifuge.

tions and receive the local officials. I spent the day
in talking to the Duchess, for all my books and work
had been left at Antwerp. I was very badly lodged
and had only my bedroom, which was dreadfully
damp.

"The gentlemen had been buying contraband
goods all day and persuaded the Duchess to do the
same in the evening. MM. de St. Aignan and de
Bondy came to fetch her in a hired carriage. The
coachman, who apparently had driven them the
evening before, thought he knew the place to which
he was to take them, so they stopped at the door
of a house and began to mount the stairs, when
the mistress of the house arrived with a light in her
hand. At the sight of this woman the gentlemen
became much embarrassed and besought the Duchess
to come downstairs again, telling her at the same time
that they had mistaken the warehouse. She kept
repeating, ' It does not matter, I will go up just the
same,' until they were obliged to admit they had
been altogether misdirected, and that this was a
house where they had acquaintances whom it was
impossible for them to present to her. The Duchess,
however, still insisted, whereupon they were obliged
to tell her that it was a house of ill-fame ; this made
her furious.

"The following morning, on leaving Bois-le-Duc,
we passed through the whole town, which is rather
pretty, and has a population of 12,000, all of whom
are Catholics.

"The road was just as ugly as on the previous day
as far as the spot where we took our lunch, and we
were unable to proceed faster than a walking pace.

" We lunched at the house of a pastor, which was remarkable for its cleanliness. From there we continued as far as Gertruidenberg, where we waited an interminable time to cross a small river in a ferry boat. While the Emperor visited the fortifications we continued our journey still at the same pace. I was with the Queen of Westphalia, who was in a very bad temper with the King, perhaps justifiably, for such a husband must make her very unhappy; I pity her sincerely.

" The road improved five leagues from Bergen-op-zoom; we thought it delightful after our experience of the last two days. Nothing but meadows, gardens, magnificent fields, and charming Dutch villages were visible. We continued our route along the Meuse by the side of the famous Moerdyk, which is an arm of the river and forms the boundary between the French Empire and Holland. There are many fortifications. Here we crossed the Meuse, which becomes very narrow, and were only 15 leagues from Amsterdam.

" What would I not have given to have been able to visit this fine capital, but when one travels with the Emperor one learns to forgo all ideas of pleasure trips.

" We were obliged to cross some more dykes in ferry boats, arriving at last at nine in the evening at Bergen-op-Zoom, which is well fortified and has from 8,000 to 12,000 inhabitants.

" The houses here were dreadful, but we were put up in the best. A wooden ladder did service for a staircase, and our apartments consisted of two rooms; nevertheless, the Emperor insisted on staying there another day. The other houses were in the same style.

" The first person I met was M. Bourdier, who had established himself in my room, furious at being left at Breda, and declaring he would send in his resignation. In vain I talked to him, I could not calm him. Presently I, too, became angry and told him to go away, because he tired me. Happily he obeyed this behest immediately, but did not expect the same fate was in store for him on the morrow.

" We sat down to dinner, at which the Emperor expressed great dissatisfaction with his quarters, so as he could not lay the blame on any of us, his wrath fell upon the dinner. At each dish he remarked, ' What a disgusting stew, if only there were a leg of mutton.' This was brought to him; then he said, ' If only there were some salad ; ' that, too, was brought. When he saw that the same thing happened each time, he retired to bed. What amused me most was the Duchesse de Montebello, who was bursting with laughter in spite of the signs I made to her. She is really not courtier enough for the country in which we live, besides, she has one great fault which will tell against her, she is too much attached to me.

" We all retired to our rooms determined to sleep the whole of the next day. The King and Queen of Westphalia found fair quarters, but without beds or chairs ; the Prince de Neuchâtel a room without any glass to the window; he was therefore obliged to use his papers to keep out the draughts !

" The Viceroy arrived too late for dinner, and was quartered on an invalid who suffered with dreadful catarrh, and who, for supper, gave him hot lemonade and bread, saying as he presented the glass, ' I cannot offer you a better, it is the one out of which I drink myself,' consequently the Viceroy was obliged to drink from it!

" I went to bed with the firm intention of not being wakened the next day. Vain hope!

" The Emperor, who apparently did not find his lodgings sufficiently attractive, mounted his horse at four o'clock and decided while riding to depart at eight, and to leave one set of attendants here. The confusion caused by this unexpected departure was so great that all the luggage was left behind!

" The Emperor refused to wait, and nearly left the King and Queen of Westphalia behind; however, they arrived just as we were embarking on the canal.

" The Viceroy had not found his quarters sufficiently comfortable, and so had slept elsewhere. Apparently he told his valet to call him late in the morning. The man had taken away his uniform and locked the door from outside. Happily the room was on the ground floor, so the Viceroy jumped from the window on to the square in somewhat light attire, to the great astonishment of the inhabitants!

" I do not know who was malicious enough to tell this story to the Emperor, but he was so furious, the Viceroy was sent back to Paris on our return to Brussels.

" At eight o'clock we proceeded through the town in our carriages and passed close by the trading port in which a great many vessels were lying. We embarked at the spot where the canal joins the Scheldt, and went down stream for an hour in some charming gondolas. The Scheldt here is more than a league in breadth and its water already tidal. The weather was very fine and calm, so our boats moved smoothly. Away to the right was the foreland of the Isle of Tholen.

" The sea air gave us such an appetite that we ate a cold lunch. I do not know what evil genius put this idea into our heads, but everybody became ill. The Queen of Westphalia and myself were the least inconvenienced because we had taken the precaution of immediately going into the fresh air. But the Emperor, the Viceroy, and the Duc d'Istrie were violently sick. They therefore determined to disembark at ten o'clock upon the Isle of Zuid-Beveland without ascertaining if there were any carriages there to convey us to the other side.

" After making inquiries the Duc d'Istrie at last found us two or three peasant conveyances which were neither carts nor carriages, and to which two horses were harnessed ; these were so high that a ladder was needed to get into them, and so narrow that two people could scarcely sit abreast ; they had no springs, consequently were very hard and, to complete our misfortunes, were occupied by a number of very disagreeable small intruders.

" The Duc d'Istrie mounted his horse and preceded us to arrange for boats to be prepared for us on the other side of the island.

" The carriage in which the Duchesse de Montebello rode with the Comtesse de Liverstein and the Viceroy capsized and was broken into a thousand pieces. He alighted on his feet, the Duchesse escaped with a tumble, but the Comtesse de Liverstein was dragged along by the horses and her elbow badly injured.

" The island of Zuid-Beveland is really charming. On the road we passed through fruit gardens and little woods of limes, elms, and willows, interspersed with small villages. In the little town of Goes we were agreeably surprised to find carriages, excellent compared with those we had just left.

" After passing through the town of Zeebourg, which is rather pretty, we arrived at the other side of the island at Hoopfort. There we embarked in a packet boat and again went down the Scheldt. We saw many porpoises, a very curious fish having the head of a pig, while its body is quite round ; it rolls on its back on the surface of the water, and in this way makes a great deal of progress in a short time.

" We disembarked at four o'clock at the head of Fort Ramshen, where the best carriages of the town of Middelburg were waiting for us. I do not exaggerate when I say they must have been constructed at least 150 years ago.

" We were so famished that we ate two large military loaves which some soldiers brought us.

" The Emperor inspected the town of Flushing on horseback, while the Queen of Westphalia and I continued our journey to Middelburg. The Island of Walcheren is just as fine as Zuid-Beveland ; should one, however, be tempted to settle there, one would soon pay very dearly. The air is so pestilential that every year during the months of September and October there are the most frightful epidemics of malarial fever, consequently the inhabitants seldom live to the age of fifty. Their complexions are yellow and livid. The Emperor is obliged to relieve the large garrison every three months, and yet two-thirds of the

soldiers are always ill when they return. It is essential
for them to drink wine while they are in the island.

" We continued our road along a very high dyke
as far as Middelburg, which we reached at five o'clock,
and were lodged in a house belonging to the Emperor,
which had formerly been a convent. It had been
decorated and furnished for our reception, hence the
papers were still quite fresh. I felt some repugnance,
however, at sleeping in the bed in which some English
had died about two years previously. I am so timid
about illness that I imagined I could still scent the
odour of death in the town. It is said more than
30,000 English perished at Middelburg during that
epidemic.

" My apartment looked upon a courtyard filled
with fine trees. We were entertained with some
delightful military music, which I would have listened
to with pleasure had it not prevented my sleeping.
My attendants ultimately arrived at three o'clock, so
I was able at last to go to bed, but they brought me
no change of clothing, consequently the Emperor will
be obliged to see me in the same dress and chemise
until we leave here.

" I resigned myself to the situation without any
fuss, but the Queen of Westphalia was inconsolable ;
her women arrived twenty-four hours after us, so she
made the unfortunate Comtesse de Liverstein stay
up all night in the antechamber to make tea for her, and
when it was brought she scolded her, would not drink
it, and cried with rage. It requires an angel from
Heaven to put up with her. I know very well what
I should have done if I had been a lady-in-waiting.

" I did not wake on the 10th till midday, when

the Emperor gave us a pleasant surprise by saying he would take us at two o'clock to the sea, and made an appointment to meet at the Fort de Haag at three o'clock. The Queen of Westphalia, however, kept me waiting more than an hour, which made me at least as impatient as herself. I was really angry to think how vexed the Emperor would be with me if I did not arrive in time, accordingly I was out of temper the whole day.

" As a rule I am a good-natured person, perhaps too weak, but when in a passion (which happens very rarely) I am perhaps more angry than other women.

" The part of the island over which we wandered is like an ornamental garden, full of fruit trees, weeping willows, elms, and, above all, most beautiful meadows and lovely flowers.

" There are few villages, but many scattered houses, extremely clean and inhabited by rich farmers. A marshy odour is perceptible everywhere, and in walking on these beautiful meadows one is often astonished to find oneself halfway to the knee in water.

" At four o'clock we reached Fort Haag, behind which are the dunes. These are sand hills of various shapes from which we could see the tips of masts which showed the sea was not far distant.

" I was impatient to see it at once, so, to while away the time, we tasted the cream, which is excellent, and is preserved in curious green bottles.

" The Emperor wished to show us the sea at once, but here the dunes were impassable, which obliged us to take another short journey of two hours, in carriages, to find a spot which we could climb. At last we found it, and I was much astonished on getting

out to find my legs half buried in sand. Each step
we took was equally troublesome, but the ascent was
nothing to travellers as intrepid as ourselves, and we
were well repaid by the fine view that burst upon us
when we reached the top of the hills.

" We saw the ocean as an immense surface of water
bounded only by the horizon; the sun was setting, and
coloured the sea like a rainbow. Far off we could
descry some fishing boats returning from their labour,
protected by a sloop. It is always necessary to
protect them in this manner from the English, who
take their fish, which they refuse to pay for. The sea
was very calm except on the shore, where it was breaking upon the rocks with some violence.

" The Emperor called for maps and talked with
the engineers.

" The Queen of Westphalia and I amused ourselves
by picking up shells with which the beach was covered.
Some were charming, but those of the Mediterranean
and the Indies are said to be infinitely finer. These
shells combined with the unwholesome air and the
mischievous trick of the King, were the cause of my
having three attacks of fever.

" In the middle of our amusement I saw that the
Viceroy and the Duc d'Istrie were watching and
laughing at us in a very significant manner. I had
not time to ask why, before the tide came up with
great force, faster than we were able to run and
wetted us to the knees; fortunately it returned as
quickly as it had come.

" These gentlemen then explained this was the
usual habit of the tide, they might, however, have been
gallant enough to warn us.

" We gave up our search and asked the Emperor's permission to change. His reply was, ' Stay as you are, ladies, this bath will do you good,' so he made us wait till eight o'clock.

" When we reached home we dined, and the same military music was performed as on the evening before.

" On the 11th, the weather was shocking all day ; this did not prevent the Emperor from going a second time to see Flushing. I remained in bed in a high fever.

" I do not know what has become of my iron constitution, it has disappeared entirely. I am sure this is the fault of the doctor, who during the whole journey has done nothing but dose me.

" On his return the Emperor told us that he had seen an English frigate approach within range of the cannon of Flushing, which in obedience to his order had bombarded her so hotly that she had retired quicker than she came.

" On the morning of the 12th, the Emperor held a council ; it really was not our fault that we heard everything, for the hall was close to my room and the Emperor shouted terribly.

" I had fever again all night, so being much fatigued and the weather dreadful, I only drove out at two o'clock to see the town.

" Middelburg has 30,000 inhabitants ; it is a fortress, surrounded by beautiful country houses and gardens, but I was unable to see them, not having our horses here. The finest buildings of the town are the Cathedral, the town hall, and the meat markets ; they are at least as fine as those I have seen in Paris, and much cleaner.

" The trading port is very large and surrounded by avenues where the people of Middelburg promenade on Sundays. Some of the houses are fine.

" On returning I found the Queen of Westphalia very much out of temper because I had not taken her, but she wearies me by her incessant inquiry, ' Do you still care for the Duchesse de Montebello ? '

" I have only known the Duchess two months, and am most attached to her, so could not help replying to the Queen, ' My dear, I do not change my friends like my chemises.' What she said to me is just the way a Queen talks. People say that women of our rank do not know how to form their attachments, but I should like to show there are exceptions. It is quite true the poor Queen is very unfortunate with her friends, hardly has she made a friend before the King makes her his mistress, and that really is not the way to keep her attached to them.

" In the evening the Viceroy took the Duchesse de Montebello to purchase contraband goods, and to see the spire of the Cathedral which is said to be very ancient.

" It was decided that we should depart the following day whatever the weather might be. I am glad, for, although the island is certainly very attractive, I have not much enjoyed wearing the same clothes for four days.

" In the evening we received the local officials. There were not very many, and most of them did not understand French."

Here the manuscript breaks off. The journey, however, was far from completed. The Emperor left Middelburg on May 13 after Mass, inspected the forts as he passed, and reached Antwerp at ten o'clock. On the 14th he left Antwerp at four in the afternoon and arrived at Laeken at nine. The 15th and 16th were spent at Laeken ; on the 15th, a play was performed at Brussels, followed by the presentation of the ladies ; on the 16th, inspection of the manufactories and a *fête* at the Hôtel de Ville ; on the 17th, Ghent was visited ; on the 18th, Bruges ; here, on the following day, Marie-Louise visited the tomb of her ancestress Marie of Burgundy, daughter of Charles the Rash and wife of Maximilian ; on the 20th, she left Bruges for Ostend by the *Wilhelmina*, a barque from Ghent ; on the 21st, she left Ostend for Dunkirk ; and on the 22nd arrived at Lille, where they stayed over the 23rd ; then Bethune, Calais, Boulogne were visited on the 25th ; Abbeville, Saint Valery, Fécamp, Dieppe, on the 26th ; the 27th–29th were spent at Le Havre, and the 30th–31st at Rouen. On June 1 at nine o'clock the Emperor returned to Saint-Cloud.

CHAPTER V

AFTER returning on June 1 to Saint-Cloud, Napoleon remained for nearly a year in the vicinity of Paris, holding his Court at the various country seats, thereby recalling the days of nomad sovereignty. Princes, princesses, the city of Paris, ministers, marshals, the Imperial Guard, all vied with one another in *fêting* the Empress. Throughout the spring there was a succession of balls, suppers, plays, and more or less lively diversions, in which entertainers like Depreaux exerted their ingenuity, preparing festivals which, while being novel and flattering, should also be interesting. It must be confessed that they were not very successful, in spite of the costumes, staging, topical allusions, and songs. Their inventions at the present time appear dismal enough, not to mention the catastrophe with which they terminated.

Victor de Broglie wrote to Marmont on July 1 :

" Our *fêtes* are finished, Monseigneur, and you have little to regret. We have had balls, fireworks, and illuminations, a few extra lamps and rockets, a few more gowns with trains, and that is all. The art of giving *fêtes* has not advanced as rapidly as the opportunities for them have increased. We found this out at the ball at the Ecole Militaire, where there were only some six or seven thousand too many people. Consequently the door had to be closed on several important persons, among whom were the Minister for War and the Minister for the Interior. The Empress danced at all these *fêtes*, and it is said she is beginning to lose all her Germanic habits ; her feet, which are two of the smallest that ever trod the pavement of Vienna, now turn outwards, and she curtsies with her head instead of her knees."

The *fêtes* were over, said Victor de Broglie ; but there was yet one more to come, viz. the one prepared for their Majesties by Prince Schwarzenberg and the Princess, *née* d'Arenberg, at the former Hôtel Montesson, in the rue de la Chaussée d'Antin. A large wooden ballroom had been constructed over the garden, which was connected with the house by a gallery, also made of wood. The ceilings were of tarpaulin, covered with varnished paper. The floors had been raised to the level of the rooms by scaffolding. An enormous chandelier in the centre, and sconces upon the walls, were designed to shed a flood of light like sunshine. The hangings consisted of thin materials, draped on the walls or suspended as curtains. The *fête* included a band of wind instruments which was to perform in the Cour d'Honneur until the arrival of their Majesties. According to the programme, the Emperor and Empress were. to pass through the concert hall into the garden, pausing in

front of the Temple of Apollo, where the Muses would
sing a chorus ; from there they would proceed by the
Allée de la Cascade to the Subterranean Grotto,
where orchestral music would be performed, thence
to the Vine Bower, adorned with monograms, garlands,
and mirrors, having a large buffet at the farther end.
Here there was to be a concert of French and German
music with solos on a new instrument, the harmonica.
Next they would come to the Temple of Fame, where
they would sit on a dais to the blare of trumpets, the
singing of choirs, and the diffusing of perfumes, till
finally their Majesties would arrive at the Imperial
Pavilion, from the platform of which they were to
witness a *fête de Château* and a *ballet champêtre* staged
like the gardens at the Laxenburg, to be followed by
fireworks. After that they were to return to the
great hall and proceed to the ballroom.

Madame de Luçay, who accompanied the Empress
and sat behind her, noticed that Prince Eugène was
whispering to the Emperor. One of the draperies in the
ballroom had just caught fire, so the Emperor rose, and
having taken the arm of the Empress as if he intended
to walk about the hall, went out by the first door.
Madame de Luçay followed by a small exit behind
the throne. In an instant all was in flames. It
seems extraordinary that so few people were killed.
There must have been a mad rush, but of this the less
said the better ! The women lost their shawls, their
necklaces, their diamond combs ; the men their
swords, their hats, their shoes ; Baron de Garzoni-
Venturi, General Doumerc, General Préval, M. de

Magnien, Baron de Torrégiant, General de Tousard, Baron de Juste, M. de Montlivault, Baron de Montesquiou, M. Pioche, and others all bemoaned the loss of their shoes on account of the buckles, a proof that these gentlemen ran away very quickly.

Princess Schwarzenberg who was crushed by the great lustre, lost 938 diamonds, weighing 269 carats ; Prince Kouratine the Russian Ambassador lost a a diamond sword mount, part of a diamond epaulette, a diamond loop from his hat, a diamond garter buckle, and a large diamond on a square snuff-box with a portrait of the Emperor of Austria. It fell to the floor and the stones dropped out. Princess Schwarzenberg was one of the first victims, but there were many others, the wife of the Russian Consul, Comtesse de la Leyen, Madame Tousard, the Préfet of Istria, and Princess de Carignan.

All this became known by rumour. Without imposing silence, great discretion was observed. This catastrophe, like that in the Place Louis XV. during the fireworks for the Dauphin's marriage, portended disaster. The Empress, from whom it was impossible to conceal the death of Princess Schwarzenberg, was deeply moved ; when on awaking next morning she heard of her death, she shed many tears.

It may have been to distract her thoughts that the Emperor took her to Rambouillet, from July 6th to the 17th. There they stayed in semi-state. The Emperor was in good spirits. He amused himself by playing rounders, and although already stout, he still ran easily enough. In one of these games he fell twice,

for as he rushed forward to seize his opponent the
Grand Maréchal, who eluded him each time, the
Emperor twice rolled on the sand four paces away
from him. There were other delightful sports.
Marie-Louise wrote :

" We celebrated the *fête* of my brother-in-law
Camille (Borghese), whom we tease almost as much as
Prince Antoine de Saxe. I made all my ladies give
him a bouquet of nettles ; I gave him a watch which
plays tunes, and at night they put a hard brush among
his sheets, with the result that with a very woeful
face he paid me an early visit this morning at eight
o'clock."

On the 17th their Majesties returned to Saint-
Cloud where their life resumed its ordinary course,
but only for a short time, for on August 2 they were
installed at the Trianon. From there the Empress
wrote to Madame de Luçay :

" I had no time yesterday to give you my com-
missions, so am writing to send you them. Will you
kindly tell the Chenille embroideress that, from
to-morrow, I will take my lesson every day from one
o'clock to two, and my drawing lesson from three to
four. I beg you also to bring me a catalogue of
Lenormand's books. The Emperor says there is no
objection to the tradesmen coming here provided I
do not see them. I beg you to pay Isabey for the two
portraits, and to order one from him in the same
costume, of the size enclosed. Nitot might frame
it in a gold border with the little coloured stones
which mean ' *Louise, je t'aime.*' ' *Louise* ' should be
in larger stones and the two other words in smaller.

I would like him to do this as quickly as possible, so that I may be able to give it as a present in about a fortnight. Please excuse my urgency."

The real Marie-Louise of the moment is expressed in that letter ; her taste for methodical planning of small occupations, her attention to economy, above all her affection for Napoleon, for whom she intended this portrait which was to be placed upon his inkstand. The Emperor must not be able to write a line without beholding his wife, without reading again the vow he had made her ; it was an obsession. But should we not put to her credit this wish to be recalled to his thought, to be constantly near him, to caress him by the continual gift of her presence ? We must certainly admit that this woman either displayed sincere feeling, or was playing an infamous comedy. One is reluctant to admit she was lying—and yet !

On the return from Trianon to Saint-Cloud an interview, on the 12th, was granted to M. de Lehndorf, who had come to announce the death of the Queen of Prussia. This woman had been unable, after provoking France and insulting the Emperor, to collect her resources or accept her reverses, and had died of failure. The Emperor and the whole Court went into mourning for her ; the first period was eleven days, the second ten. All mourning would be suspended on the coming *fête* days. The Queen of Prussia had to stand aside. The 15th was the Emperor's birthday, and on this occasion the Colonne Vendôme was uncovered without any ceremony, out of consideration to the new Empress. All Paris was afoot from six in

the morning when volleys of artillery were fired. On
waking, the Emperor was greeted by the Empress
and the princes and princesses of the family, who
offered him their congratulations in his private apartments. At midday in the throne-room he received
persons of exalted rank, officers of the household and
diplomatic service. After that he attended Mass
with the *Te Deum*. The great ceremony followed
when the Emperor on his throne received deputations from Holland and Illyria. In the evening there
was a Court function with a concert on the terrace,
salutes of artillery, illuminations, and fireworks.

The birthday of the Empress, ten days later, was
celebrated in quite a different way, less formally and
with more elegance. On Saturday the 25th at one
o'clock, all the ladies of the Palace with the Duchess
and the wives of the high officials and ministers, presented their congratulations to her, and were followed
by the gentlemen. On the Sunday there was Mass
as usual, and the Emperor held a large reception which
the Empress did not attend. After dining *en famille*,
their Majesties drove through the illuminated park
and saw the fountains playing under coloured lights.
They then proceeded to the play, where *Athalie* was
given first, followed by *La Fête du Château*, with birthday odes which constituted the chief attraction of the
evening. *By Order of His Majesty, the King and
Emperor*, this compliment in the form of a vaudeville
had been specially composed by Alissan de Chazel,
who during three reigns fawned upon any one who
could pay him. It was to be performed by Ellevion

H

of the Théâtre Feydeau, Madame Decosta, pupil of the Conservatoire, M. Hippolyté from the Théâtre du Vaudeville, M. Baptiste Cadet from the Théâtre Français, Madame Gavaudan from the Théâtre Feydeau, Madame Festa from the Théâtre Bouffon, and Mdlle. Mars from the Théâtre Français. The principal artists, Mme. Gavaudan, Mme. Festa, and Mdlle. Mars, represented the three Louises, French, Italian, and German. The scene was laid in the castle of M. de Valmont. Other characters were Factotum, steward to M. de Valmont, his son Benjamin who stuttered, and Madame de Valmont, who wishing to celebrate this great occasion (Louise's birthday) promised a *dot* to any young woman of the village who bore the name Louise and possessed one of the talents of her sovereign. This offer gave an opportunity for a varied display : Louise, the French girl, had painted a portrait of the Sovereign ; Luigia sang her praises to the air of M. Paër, and Louisa *to a German melody*. M. de Valmont gave a sum of money to each of them, whereupon the theatre opened displaying a magic picture of the gardens of Schönbrunn, with the bust of Louise surrounded by villagers and others who did homage to her: ALL Germans ! Brothers !! Brothers !!! There was much singing and dancing, and the play was printed at the Imperial Press.

After these *fêtes* the only event of the month was the presentation of Bernadotte and Mdlle. Clary his wife, now Prince and Princess of Sweden. The details of the ceremony had been repeatedly revised in order to satisfy the Prince de Pontecorvo, who received from the Emperor the crown of Spain together with a million in money. He wanted two million ; but not even that sum could prevent him from turning traitor.

On September 25 the Emperor left for Fontainebleau, where on the 30th, the Mayor presented the customary offerings (*fruits d'honneur*) at the grand audience after Mass. The chief event of this visit, which lasted from October 30 to November 16, was the amazing ceremony of November 4 which was intended to pave the way for the official announcement of the pregnancy of the Empress. Napoleon desired on this occasion that all the children whom he had proposed to name after Joséphine should be baptised and that Marie-Louise should be their godmother. This was a matter of great difficulty. Thus, for instance, as there was a prince of the Imperial family, a bed had to be provided for him according to the precedent established at the baptism of Hortense's son in the year XIII. It followed that beds had to be supplied for the twenty-six other children, a veritable dormitory. Again, these beds differed greatly in size, some of the children being five, six, seven, and even ten years old, while others, like Berthier's son, were only two months old, or three like the daughter of Maret. This disparity in ages necessitated different treatment and clothing. The prescribed costume was uniformly white, and consisted of a long robe with a sash, similar to that worn by neophytes. The mothers, who were of the highest rank in the Empire, naturally vied with one another in elegance, and the long cambric robes were trimmed with none but the finest laces. Then, when everything appeared to be settled, after his Imperial Highness had been provided with a cot and one pillow, drapery, counterpane, and canopy of silver cloth ; when fifteen cradles covered with blue taffeta had been prepared for the infants to be laid on a table 30 ft. long by 3 wide, covered in its turn with a blue velvet cloth fringed with gold ; when two smaller tables with similar covers had been prepared for the double (baptismal) gifts—all had to be altered. The Emperor objected to blue, everything must be in white !

Next Fesch intervened and demanded a chrism cloth of lace $1\frac{1}{2}$ ft. wide, which would be the perquisite of the Master of Ceremonies of the Chapel. The chrism cloth was purchased. Fesch then requested that it should be carried on a bowl and not upon a cushion. The taper garnished with white velvet and silver fringes had to be of a special shape. All this was nothing. At the same time he would not dispense with the minutest ceremonial, so the ritual for catechumens had to be carried out to the smallest detail. If of suitable age the children must themselves reply to the questions of the celebrant. In each case it would be necessary for the Emperor and Empress to enter and leave the sanctuary, in order to move from one State chair to another, as the State chairs could not be moved without their canopies. The ceremony would last three or more hours. Were the children to go hungry during all this time ? The nurses would be required to be in attendance on the cots in the hall, the chapel, and elsewhere. Each time the Grand Almoner raised these points, the Emperor decided them. Although addicted to ceremony, he was anxious not to fatigue the Empress. Again on reflection, all this array of cots and nurses and the feeding of the children in his palace disgusted him, so he decided to have only one cot for the Prince. The ladies and the nurses must go straight into the chapel. " Whatever was necessary for the children's requirements could be arranged in a side chapel."

Finally, after twenty changes and an epic fight between the Chief Almoner and the Master of Ceremonies, the programme was settled, and was to have been printed at Fontainebleau, but the time was too short. Written programmes had to suffice. Invitations were despatched to Princes, Princesses, high officials, to the Ordinary and Extraordinary officers of every household ; to Senators, and State Councillors, individually ; all were to be in full costume, with plumed hats and cloaks. The ceremony was to take place at midday ; at half-past eleven the children were to be in the chapel with their mothers, and for those who had none, substitutes must be provided. The chapel had been divided into two parts by a balustrade ; the first, comprising the nave, contained the State chairs with prie-Dieu for their Majesties ; the second, converted into a sanctuary, also contained canopied chairs of State for the Emperor and Empress as well as an armchair for the Grand Almoner, chairs for the Cardinals, and benches for the Archbishops and Bishops. Six feet in front of the altar was a table on which were placed the font (a big silver gilt bowl found among the Palace silver), credences for the gifts, and the ewer and basin.

As on the most important occasions the procession moved into the icy chapel with its marble pavement. The Prince (second son of Hortense, who died in 1831 during the Insurrection of the Papal States), in charge of his governess, immediately preceded the Emperor and Empress, and was placed on the right of the Imperial prie-Dieu. Every one was standing. The Grand Almoner, with his head covered, approached the balustrade and asked the Emperor, " What child are you presenting to the Church ? " In the reply the number of children, boys and girls, was stated. " What names do you give these children ? " The Emperor held out the list of names, to save the situation. Many of the children present were but a few months old and should have been Josephine's god-children and named Joseph or Josephine, *e.g.* the daughters of Beauharnais, Caffarelli, Defrance, Legrange, and the sons of Becker, Colbert, Curial, Duchâtel, Maret, Turenne. This silent list averted awkward reminiscences.

Facing each child the Grand Almoner proceeded with the preparatory ceremonies, whereupon their Majesties entered the Sanctuary and sat upon their chairs of State opposite the font. The children, led or carried by their mothers, were placed right and left. The lady-in-waiting uncovered the Prince's head and went with him to the font, which was the signal for each mother to do the same for her child. After the Mass and the Benediction, the Grand Chamberlain and the Grand Marshal served their Majesties for the ceremonial washing. After the Bishops had done homage the procession formed again and returned to the drawing-room, where the Empress presented the mothers with lockets containing the portraits of the Emperor by Isabey, surrounded with brilliants, worth from six to eight thousand francs each. In the evening, *L'Enlèvement des Sabines* was performed and a Court reception held in the State apartments.

This ceremony celebrated the declaration of the pregnancy, which the Emperor notified officially to the Senate and the Emperor of Austria. He was really in love with the Empress, and was foolishly lavish to any one who assisted in displaying her beauty. Duplan, for instance, for whose posterity was reserved such strange destinies and who was alone, in Napoleon's opinion, capable of dressing the Empress's hair, received a present of 12,000 frs. over and above his salary of 12,000 frs. and 6000 frs. pension. Canova was summoned to make a statue of Marie-Louise, for which he was given 30,000 frs. Napoleon did everything in his power to obliterate traces of his first wife's existence. Her figure was removed from David's *Distribution des Aigles ;* he would have liked to take it out of Regnault's *Mariage du Roi de Westphalie.* Joséphine's monogram was removed from the great and small apartments of the Tuileries.

The Grand Marshal occupied an apartment next

to that of the Empress, but was moved in order to give more room for the wardrobe apartments. The Emperor overwhelmed her with small attentions, and the Théâtre des Petits Appartements, where the Opéra Comique was usually given, was designed to enliven her Majesty. Furthermore, she followed the chase in the forest of Vincennes, in the plain of Freminville, in the forest of St. Germain, and in all the environs of Paris to which the Emperor betook himself for hunting, until the time arrived when the state of her health prevented her driving in a carriage, she had then to content herself with walking on the terrace beside the water, followed by her ladies and the officers and pages. Sometimes, as on March 10, the Empress walked for an hour in the garden, when the paths, terraces, and avenues were thronged with an immense crowd, attracted by the hope of seeing her. After that the Emperor ordered his architect Fontaine to construct an underground passage, to connect the apartments in the castle with the terrace, without obstructing the public. Everything was prepared, down to the barrels for supplying wine to the fountain in the Place du Châtelet. "This device was not to be announced beforehand, but was to appear un-expectedly." Pages were to be sent to announce the event to the Municipal Body. If a Prince should arrive, the lucky messenger would receive a pension of ten thousand francs for the rest of his life. Cardinal Maury became agitated over the mandate he was to deliver and begged for the order of the ceremonial to be communicated to him. Of more importance still was the Virgin's shirt. Since the ninth century the church of Notre-Dame de Chartres had possessed a relic of the Virgin deposited there by Charles the Bald. This relic was to be exposed with great solemnity throughout the prayers which were to be offered up for her Majesty's happy delivery. On March 14 the Chapter, headed by the Bishop of Versailles, presented the Empress with a facsimile of this precious relic in embroidered satin, for it had been the immemorial custom to send six deputies with a similar copy to the Queens and Dauphines upon their first confinement.

On March 19 the labour pains began. On the 20th the baby was born and privately baptised. On the 21st the Emperor, seated on his throne, received the homage of the Court ; on the 22nd, the homage of the "Grand Corps de l'Etat," to whom his Majesty the King of Rome gave audience ; on the 24th there was a grand parade in the Cour des Tuileries ; on the 25th the last bulletin was published, to the effect that her Majesty the Empress had safely passed through all complications. Everything had already been prepared for the removal of the young mother to Saint-Cloud, which took place exactly a month after her confinement. From May 9 the Empress followed the chase in her carriages, until on May 14, as though completely recovered, she left for Rambouillet, which she left on the 22nd for Normandy. By five o'clock the company were in their carriages ; *déjeûner* was taken at the Château de Tubœuf with Comte de Lillers (Chamberlain since the great promotion), a halt was made to inspect the

Pin stables ; the party slept at Caen, where the Hôtels d'Aigrefeuille and de Fresne, in the Rue Guilbert, had been combined to provide a palace. M. de Nathan, formerly Marquis, commanded the Mounted Guard of Honour.

All went well, there were neither benefits nor favours, scarcely any audiences, save for the old nobility. M. de Courville commanded the foot guards ; M. de Vandœuvre presided over the Electoral College ; and M. Lentaigne de Logivière was Mayor of Caen. Smiles, presents, and pensions were pressed upon them, thirty-seven ladies of Caen were presented, but all of these had the prefix " de " ; only gentlemen were admitted to the levée on the 25th. Money, indeed, was liberally bestowed on the poor at Houdan, Dreux, Laigle, Argentan, and at Falaise. Caen, for example, received 20,000 frs. for the hospitals, 100,000 frs. were allotted to the victims of the fires at Evrechy and 700,000 for the canal from Caen to the sea. Everywhere, as far as Cherbourg, the same liberality prevailed. An inexhaustible stream of gold flowed from the hands of the Emperor ; gold, however, is not everything, and the bourgeois knew it.

Marie-Louise appeared haughty, bored, and silent, in the mocking Norman phrase a " *tête de bois.*" She could not find a word to say to the officials, nor a smile for the little girls who offered her flowers. She took part languidly in the receptions, balls, and promenades, while her lady-in-waiting distributed the necessary gifts, like an alms, in a dry contemptuous voice. The Empress only relaxed at Cherbourg, and even then not at the performances given by Feydeau's company, but in excursions with the Emperor, when visiting the ships or the shore or when in rough horseplay he treated her as a comrade.

But granting that she seemed to be inert and incapable of making herself agreeable, might it not have been in consequence of the imprudence of undertaking this journey in which she desired to accompany her husband though hardly recovered from her confinement rather than to her timidity and disposition ? The fatigue she endured was apparent from her emaciation, for she insisted on going about with the Emperor, and the Emperor was indefatigable. On several occasions they started at four in the morning. On the first day they travelled for nineteen hours, from four in the morning to eleven at night. Twice the stages of their journey lasted twelve hours. This was nothing in comparison with the 1808 tour from which Joséphine, with all her strength and powers of resistance, escaped with only a serious illness ; but Marie-Louise was a very young woman, exhausted by her confinement. They were no sooner back from Cherbourg than the rush began again, intensified, doubled and trebled, for the baptism of the King of Rome.

On June 8-9 several State functions were held, also a kind of Imperial *fête* at the Hôtel de Ville ; followed by a series of *fêtes* at Saint-Cloud for the army, the people, and the Court. The last took place in a terrific storm, which drenched everything, including the spectators, from head to foot, likewise the tents under which they were to sup, and finally the dishes that were to have been served to them.

From Saint-Cloud they went on to Trianon. The mistress of the robes wrote :

" I arrived at Trianon about nine o'clock, just when they were sitting down to table, but as their Majesties were dining at the Hameau and walked about until they retired, we, Madame de Brignole, Madame de Lobau, and I, were forgotten in the *salon de service* the whole evening."

After having spent a week at Trianon, and a week at Rambouillet, they returned to Saint-Cloud and proceeded to Paris for the Emperor's birthday. On the 25th, however, they were back at Trianon, in order that the Emperor might concentrate his energies on the birthday of the Empress. Accordingly, after Mass, their Majesties drove through the park where all the fountains were playing. In the evening, after a very uninteresting day, the guests arrived punctually at eight o'clock, the men in silk clothes, the ladies in short dresses ; they waited in the salons and in the gallery of the State room, where the heat was so great that several ladies fainted. At half-past nine the Emperor and Empress came out of their private room and held a reception, after which every one retired to the gardens. The illuminated *parterres* were duly admired, and then every one adjourned to the theatre to see *Les Projets de Mariage* and *La Grande Famille,* an incredibly silly topical trifle of M. Alissan de Chazet. After this the company proceeded along a course marked out with lamps, coloured glasses, and burning faggots, to hear a cantata at the Pavillon Français, and to see a roundabout manned by children in Chinese costume, a children's dance round the statue of Venus and an act out of the Opera, consisting of a country wedding, clowns, acrobats, peasants, dances and games. Afterwards supper was served on little tables at the Grand Trianon.

From Trianon they went to Compiègne, where Marie-Louise had the pleasure of following coursing on horseback. Her health, however, had not improved, and she suffered from frequent chills and fever. As she refused to be separated from her husband, she would not admit she was ill and continued to live the strange timeless existence in which Napoleon, lord of the hour, declined to admit that he could be its slave.

"The Emperor is to leave to-night," wrote Ségur, on September 1, "the Empress on Saturday, about two hours after midnight. . . . We are to rejoin the Emperor at Antwerp and then to visit Utrecht, Amsterdam, Le Texel, Alkmaer, The Hague, Rotterdam, Flushing, and Fontainebleau. . . . I have seen no journey arranged and published beforehand as this has been. There will have to be some alterations in the dates unless things have changed considerably."

CHAPTER VI

THE JOURNEY OF 1811

THIS journey can only be understood by comparing the Emperor's itinerary from September 19-30, 1811.

Sept. 19. Departure from Compiègne, 3.30 a.m. Arrival at Montreuil, 4 p.m. Review at Boulogne, 8 p.m., where he slept.

,, 20. Boulogne : Review. Visit to the Fleet. By sea to Wimereux and Ambleteuse.

,, 21. Boulogne : Review.

,, 22. Boulogne : Reviews and Inspections. Departure for Calais, Dunkirk, Furnes at midnight.

,, 23. Departure from Furnes, 1 a.m. Arrival at Ostend, 3 p.m. Review. Visit to the town. Breske, 6 p.m.

,, 24. Visit to the fortifications of Ile de Cadzeaud and the squadron lying off Flushing. Slept on board the *Charlemagne*.

,, 25-26. On board the *Charlemagne*.

,, 27. At Flushing : Reception of Authorities. Visit to the Works.

,, 28. From Flushing to Middelburg and Veere.

,, 29. From Flushing up the Scheldt again, arrival at Antwerp, 1 a.m.

,, 30. At Antwerp, audiences. Arrival of Marie-Louise from Brussels at 4 o'clock.

Although Marie-Louise kept no journal of her travels in 1811, she made ample amends for this hiatus in a series of confidential letters.

Their Majesties reached Compiègne on August 30, 1811, and their arrival coincided with the death of General Ordener, the Governor of the Palace. In spite of a slight attack of biliousness and a nervous chill which affected her hands and feet, her Majesty mounted her horse to follow the chase, and was present at the Comédie. With his usual punctiliousness on points of etiquette, the Emperor laid down the strictest injunctions as to presentations and ceremonial for State functions. He departed on the night of the 18th at 3 a.m. In the afternoon the Empress made a long expedition to Pierrefonds. " Some fine ruins were there with which I was not acquainted, and the part of the forest which led to them was most sombre, almost rivalling the ruin in antiquity." Thus wrote Madame de Luçay to her husband. The Empress subsequently wrote to the Emperor, who had already reached Boulogne :

"Compiègne, Sept. 19, 1811.

" I am very sad, my dear, to think that instead of talking to you I must have recourse to my pen, and it needs all my courage not to give way entirely to the sorrow your departure causes me ; at this moment I am more than fifty leagues from you, and each day will increase the distance between us. You cannot imagine the feelings I have when I pass by your room and see the windows and shutters closed. You must love as I love you to understand this.

I beg you, dear one, to be careful of your health. If, to the uneasiness I feel, were added the anxiety of knowing that you were ill, I could not bear it.

" Your son is well. I have just come from him. Madame de Montesquiou said that as (I) was giving you news of him, she would not trouble you with a letter. I intend to leave on Saturday at four o'clock, and hope to reach Brussels about midnight. I have not yet written to Princess Pauline who wanted to go there too, because I did not know if you would like it. I beg you to send me your decision. In half an hour I shall be going to the play, while all my thoughts will be at Boulogne.

"Send me news of you very often. I love you very tenderly. Do not forget her who calls herself till death,

" Your tender and affectionate wife and friend,

" LOUISE."

The Comédie, that evening, performed for her Majesty, *Le Parleur Contrarié* with Dumas, Baptiste senior, Thénard, Devigny, Baptiste junior, Mmes. Mars and Demerson in the cast ; and *Les Héretiers* with Devigny, Michot, Baptiste junior, Armand, Laeair, Thénard, Mmes. Thénard and Mars. The impression made on Marie-Louise is recorded in her letter of the 20th.

"Compiègne, Sept. 20, 1811.

" I am waiting with great impatience, my dear, for news of your arrival at Boulogne. By this time you must be very busy with the fleet and with your troops, and I greatly fear that your Army may make

THE EMPRESS MARIE-LOUISE.

(From a miniature in the possession of Sir Morgan Crofton, Bart.)

you forget your tender Louise, whereas I, who am all alone, think of you incessantly. I feel our separation much more. The day that I receive your first letter will be a day of happiness for me, but I shall be yet more happy when you give me the order to rejoin you. I reckon the hours and minutes to that moment.

"I am well, so is your son who lay laughing to-day for more than half an hour on my bed. He slept well, but he is a little pale as he is cutting his teeth.

"We are beginning to have very bad weather. I offer prayers that it may not continue, as I fear the adverse winds may keep you longer on board your squadron than I could wish ; but take care, my dear one, for at the end of the week I charge you to let me come to you, be it even in the costume of a page or on horseback, no matter what, so long as I see you again.

"Prince Schwarzenberg left this morning overwhelmed with your kindness, of which he spoke last night with great appreciation.

"I went to the play where two very gay pieces were given, but far from making me laugh, they produced quite the opposite effect !

"I made an expedition yesterday with the ladies to Pierrefonds, but did not enjoy it for you were not with me. To-day I shall receive all the persons connected with this journey to say 'good-bye' to them, and to-morrow I shall go to Laeken.

"I beg you, my dear one, to write to me soon and at great length. I embrace you most tenderly in my thoughts, and am longing to tell you in person how greatly I love and cherish you.

"Your very affectionate and faithful wife,
"LOUISE."

I

The Empress duly set out on the 21st.

" The Grand Chamberlain and Béarn, Cornelissen, Saint-Aignan, Canouville, Phillipe de Ségur and Mesdames Lauriston, Aldobrandini, Brignoles, MM. d'Heriçey and Beauharnais, all accompanied the Empress to Laeken. Undoubtedly we shall make no stay there, seeing that the Emperor has forty-eight hours' start of us. The talk is all of Amsterdam," wrote Ségur.

When they had safely arrived, the Empress wrote :

"Laeken, Sept. 22, at 1 in the morning.

" MY DEAR ONE (*Mon cher ami*),
         " I have just arrived at Laeken and am not in the least tired after the journey ; we were not too hot, but the dust was frightful, such as I have never seen before. Your kind letter arrived too late for me to be able to execute your orders. I asked the gentlemen if it would be possible to remain at Valenciennes. They told me that it was too late to make the necessary arrangements. I will reply to you at greater length to-morrow. I embrace you thousands and thousands of times and am going to bed. My last thought as I fall asleep will be of you.
         " Your tender and faithful wife,
                           " LOUISE."

They had indeed arrived, but after what adventures !

" The fast coach of the Martins and the Lisettes broke down as soon as it left Compiègne," wrote Ségur. " The ladies implored me to give them the men-servants of the Castle as waiting-maids; the plate-waggon had broken down mid-way on the journey; Bausset was in despair, furious at his lodging, but unable to find any one to complain to, for we arrived at two in the morning, and despite the remarkable figure of our préfet, every one was so occupied with his own affairs and with the ladies that he was not noticed. Besides, I had all the lights put out quickly so that peevish people might get to bed without making comparisons between their own lot and that of others."

Marie-Louise had a pleasanter journey than her Lisettes. She wrote:

"Laeken, Sept. 22, 1811, at 4 o'clock.

"MY DEAR ONE,
    "I was delightfully surprised on waking to find a letter from you. You must know how happy I always am to get your letters, since I see that you think of me sometimes. The letter you wrote on the evening of the 19th only reached me as I left Compiègne. This delay annoyed me very much, for it prevented me from carrying out your wishes about my journey. I assure you, my love, that I have not been over tired and that I slept without waking from Mons, where I dined, to Laeken. I pity you if you have a dust like this on your journey for it is as black as coal. Still I have not coughed at all, and am so little fatigued that, if I could and dared rejoin you, I would start again at once. I implore you not to forget your promise to be with me at the end of the week.

" The time passes very slowly without you, and if this separation were to last many more days I should become ill with sorrow.

" To-morrow I shall receive the authorities and the ladies and in the evening I shall go to the play. I will try to be charming since this gives you pleasure, but it will be difficult for me when my heart is so heavy.

" Don't forget to give me the money you have promised me, for I shall need it at Brussels.

" I hope you will not go chasing the English a second time. Since then I wish them more ill than ever, for they were the cause of detaining you another day, and will perhaps still keep you some days at Boulogne ; but if you break your promises to me I shall not forgive you so quickly. Please let me have news of you regularly, and be sure I shall not let a day pass without writing to you, and without giving you an account of all my actions. Adieu, my dear one, I pray that your health may not suffer from the fatigues of your journey and that I may soon have the happiness of embracing you in person.

" Your faithful and tender wife,
" LOUISE."

Next day she wrote :

"Laeken, Sept. 23, at 11¼ in the morning.

" MY DEAR ONE,
" You always provide me with a charming awakening. At half-past nine to-day I received your kind letter of the 22nd. I saw with pleasure that you were leaving for Ostend, accordingly I may have news of you more rapidly. A thousand pardons if I vexed

you by saying that you were forgetting me in the midst of military operations. I realise, love, that I reproached you very unjustly, nevertheless, I believe you could never think of me as much as I think of you, for my mind is occupied with you day and night. I am wonderfully well. Yesterday I took a pretty drive in the environs of Laeken. To-day before dinner I shall receive the authorities and the ladies and then shall go to the play. For dinner I have invited Mme. d'Ursel, Mme. d'Arenberg, Mme. de la Tour du Pin, and the Commandant of the Guard of Honour, who is the husband of Mme. de Trasegnies. I have also received Mme. de Croix, who has arrived, and Mme. de Mun the wife of the Chamberlain, who was suggested to me by M. de Montesquiou, because she is the wife of the Mayor. Please write and tell me if I am to receive Mme. de Cornelissen, who is the only chamberlain's wife who has not yet made her curtsey. This evening I shall wear a rose-coloured gown because I know you like it, and I love to please you from afar. Adieu, my love, I embrace you many times in thought, and promise you to be so amiable to the Belgians, that you will have reason to be pleased with me.

"Your tender and faithful friend and wife,

"LOUISE."

She herself describes her journey on the 23rd :

"Château de Laeken, Sept. 24, at 10 in the morning.

"MY DEAR ONE,

"How happy I am to see by your charming letter of this morning that you are so near me; I now desire nothing more fervently than to receive

the despatch in which you tell me to rejoin you. I
shall then make great haste. I am much more at ease
now that I know that you are well. Do not be uneasy,
my dear ; the dust has not done me the slightest harm
and I did not get catarrh. Now all danger from the
dust is over, for rain has fallen in torrents all the
afternoon.

" Yesterday very few ladies came to my reception.
Most of them are in the country or laid up, but those
who came to be presented to me had good manners
and were well dressed.

" Yesterday I went to the play where they gave
Felix and *La Mélomanie*. I have never seen a worse
performance. They sang out of tune and acted very
badly, but to-morrow Talma is to play in *Andromaque*.
In the evening I shall have a concert and card games.
The misery among manufacturers is excessive, and
they have been obliged to discharge two-thirds of
their workmen ; they are doing no business at all.
The Préfet told me of this in such a manner that I
could not help promising to make many purchases.
I hope you will be so good as to pay for them, for
travelling is ruinous to one's clothes and one's finances.
They told me that before I arrived the work-women
prayed to God for three days that I would relieve
their misery, for otherwise they would have no bread
this winter. Among other articles they have made,
two coverlets were brought to me, but they are too
expensive. I sent them word that these must be
kept until I was brought to bed with my second son,
and you know that I am in no great haste for his
arrival. Yesterday I received tidings of your son
who has arrived quite safely at Saint-Cloud with his

accustomed gaiety. Adieu, dear love, I hope the weather will clear up again so as not to delay the moment when I shall have the pleasure of seeing you. I write from my bed in which I am resting, because I know you are pleased when I do so.

" Your faithful and affectionate wife and friend,
" MARIE-LOUISE."

What impression did the Empress make upon the public who saw her at the play ? She arrived punctually at eight o'clock, in very full dress, which consisted of a high diadem of jewels, sprays of the same, and a diamond necklace. The front of her pink satin gown was embroidered with diamonds, and on the left side with coloured stones imitating a shaded bouquet. When she made three curtseys on reaching the front of the box, the enthusiasm of the Belgians became delirious, also on another occasion when she appeared at the play with a bouquet of tulips in her hand, there was a fight for the scattered petals. All went well so long as she was not obliged to speak, but she was less successful in the drawing-room.

Mme. de la Tour de Pin, wife of the Préfet de la Dyle, wrote :

" We were invited to Laeken every day to spend the evening and play Loto, which lasted for about a week and was very tiresome. The Empress was dull to a degree and her demeanour never varied. Each day she made the same remark asking me to feel her pulse : ' Do you think I am feverish ? ' I invariably replied : ' Madame, I know nothing about it.' A few men came in to make a little conversation while we were taking tea, among others, Maréchal Mortier and M. de Béarn. It was the duty of the Duc d'Ursel in his capacity of Mayor, to suggest the morning's excursion according to the weather. One day when visiting the Museum, Marie-Louise appeared to notice a fine portrait of her illustrious grandmother, Maria-Theresa. The Duc d'Ursel proposed that it should be placed in her drawing-room at Laeken, but she replied : ' Oh ! certainly not ; the frame is too old.' On another occasion he suggested as an interesting place to visit, that part of the forest of Soignies that is known by the name of the pilgrimage of the Arch-Duchesse Isabelle, whose saintliness and goodness are cherished in the hearts of the people. She replied that she did not care for woods."

Marie-Louise made the same impression on every one. Mme. de Mérode emerged from her retreat to appear at the Empress' dinner. (She was afraid of horses to which she was not accustomed, and had had a bay horse dyed black to match one of her own.) This Mme. de Mérode remarked : " The Princess, who was very young at the time and had been brought up very quietly, like all the Arch-Duchesses, had very little self-possession and knowledge of the world ; she appeared timid and embarrassed." At dinner, she sat on the right of the State chair prepared for the Emperor ; Mme. de Mérode on the left. Would not that be enough to petrify a bourgeois dinner, even more an Imperial party ? It was not only a question of these Belgian guests, there were other people there.

"MY DEAR ONE,

"I have this instant returned from Brussels, where I have been to see the Cathedral Church and the lace manufactories, and as an express messenger is setting out, I hasten to write to you to tell you I am very well and constantly thinking of you. Princess Pauline arrived at Brussels in the morning of the day before yesterday. She did not inform me of her arrival. I sent very early yesterday morning to inquire after her, but received no reply. Finally she announced her arrival and asked me for news of you. I wrote to her this morning to ask for hers and to tell her what I knew of you. She replied she was too unwell to leave her bed, that she was so ill she could not come to see me and was very badly lodged at the inn. I thought you would not object to my suggesting that she should come here to live with me. An hour later I sent a chamberlain to her, who returned with the answer that she had left for Antwerp. I send you all these details because I was told that she declined to receive the persons of my suite and was angry with me. She refused to admit Prince Aldobrandini, and I fear that, as she will see you before I do, she will say I have been impolite to her, so I prefer to tell you myself what I have done. I acted moreover on the advice of M. de Montesquiou and consulted him before inviting her to stay with me, he strongly endorsed my suggestion and is as astonished as I am at her conduct.

"Please forgive me for wearying you with these trifles, but being so afraid lest you should scold me or be displeased, I preferred to tell you the whole story. I hope you think of me sometimes in spite of your numerous engagements. I embrace you many times and am going to dress, for I am dining an hour earlier on account of the *fête*.

" Your faithful and tender wife,
" MARIE-LOUISE."

This strange episode of Princess Pauline's journey to Brussels remained unknown to the gazetteers, and her journey to Antwerp alone was mentioned. There can, however, be no doubt about it; Marie-Louise wrote on the 26th :

" Laeken, Sept. 26, at 9½, morning.

" My DEAR ONE,
" Yesterday I received your kind letter of the 24th which distressed me very much, because I see from it that you were tired and wet through. I beseech you, my love, to spare yourself a little more. You can hardly believe how much your mode of life disturbs me and torments me ; should I hear that you were ill and could not see you, I do not know what would happen to me. I am astonished you do not receive my letters regularly for I write every day, indeed were I not afraid of wearying you I should do so every hour. I am wonderfully well ; I shall go to-day to the *fête* the town is preparing for me, which consists of a comedy and a ball. I am having a gown adorned with diamonds because I know you like me to be well dressed. I shall not dance ; I hope you will not mind this.

" We are having very high winds, so I hope you will not remain with the fleet. I am frozen, for the doors and windows do not fit, and it rains in torrents.

Yesterday I received news of your son, who is well, and is beginning to take soup. The Duc and Duchesse de Bassano passed through yesterday on their way to Antwerp. I kept them to dinner. Write to me soon, my dear, that you are at Antwerp and that I am to rejoin you. I am longing for the moment when I can embrace you and tell you in person how much I love you.

"Your faithful and tender wife and friend,

"MARIE-LOUISE."

Next day she wrote :

"Laeken, Sept. 27, at 3 in the afternoon.

"MY DEAR ONE,

"Your letter of the 25th fills me with joy, the more so as I did not receive one yesterday, which was beginning to make me very uneasy. I pray that your health may always be as good. This is certainly not selfishness, for if I consulted my own feelings, I should want you to be so sea-sick that you would be obliged to return very quickly to Antwerp. I have a most lively desire to see you again. I am very well and quite comfortable at Laeken, but not so well as when I am near you. The *fête* was very fine yesterday, the company very well chosen, and the park splendidly illuminated. At the beginning they gave the little opera, *Maison à Vendre*, which was so badly sung that my poor ears are still suffering. Thank you for having thought of me, and for sending money for my purse so that I shall be able to give a larger sum to the poor. The lace-workers are delighted with the orders you have given, and the Préfet equally so, for he says they can find no one to purchase their laces.

" To-day I shall have a concert and a reception. I will try to please the Belgians, but for me every day that I pass away from you causes me so much sorrow, that, although I try to hide it, I am sure it can be easily read in my face. Adieu, my dear one, I embrace you tenderly.

" Your faithful and tender wife,
" Marie-Louise."

The total of the bill for the laces purchased for the use of her Majesty at Brussels between September 23 and 29, amounted to 134,662 frs. 59 c. In addition the Empress expended 89,145 frs. 59 c. on lace for her wardrobe department, and according to an estimate signed by her on July 29, 1812, she spent an amount equivalent to 45,519 frs. in presents. The names upon the estimate are as follows :

	Frs.
To Mme. de Montesquiou, Governess to the Children of France, 1 robe at	4,900
To Mme. de Montebello, Lady-in-Waiting 1 robe at	5,000
4 ells superfine Bruxelles at 430 frs.	1,720
6 ells	330
5 ells	165
6 ells	504
4½ ells	203.58
3 ells	144
6 ells	252
6 ells	252
6 ells	240

Frs.

To Mme. de Luçay, Lady of the Wardrobe,
1 robe 3,000
To Mme. de Mesgriny, Under-governess,
1 veil 1,320
To the Ladies-in-Waiting, 1 cape and 8
ells needle point 2,150
To the Ladies-in-Waiting, 1 veil, 3 capes 5,160
To a Lady-in-Waiting, 1 cape 1,440
To M. Bourdier, physician, 1 pair of
sleeve ruffles 430
To M. Ballouhey, treasurer, 1 pair of
sleeve ruffles 960
To the premières femmes, Ells Bruxelles
and Malines 4,191
For the journey, 6 ells Dentelles Bruxelles 528
The remainder for the journey.

Accordingly, Mme. de Montebello received one-
third of the lace presented, and we may well believe
her portion would be the most sumptuous.

" Château de Laeken, Sept. 28, 10¼ o'clock.

" MY DEAR ONE,
" I am very happy to-day, for in addition to
receiving your letters of the 26th and 27th you give
me the hope of seeing you again. I do not know what
presentiment tells me that to-morrow will be the
happy day. I await this moment with extraordinary
impatience. I assure you your absence has made me
suffer greatly and has caused me much sorrow. I am
delighted I did not know beforehand that the sea was
stormy on the 26th, for I should have imagined you

in danger and been very worried. I thank Heaven that you have not suffered from the sea. It is evident that you are fortunate in everything. I cannot understand why you do not receive my news, for I write to you most regularly, once and sometimes twice a day. So you see, dear love, it is not my fault. I am wonderfully well notwithstanding the damp and the unfavourable time of year. Yesterday I held a reception and heard some very pretty music at the concert. The Queen of Naples has not yet arrived here, but should she come to-day, as you have left it to me to decide how I will receive her, I shall at once invite her to take up her abode at the Château de Laeken. I shall remain at home this evening with the people to whom I have given the *entrée* to the Château. I embrace you many times, and hope to-day to receive word from you where I am to meet you.

 " Your faithful and affectionate wife,
                        " MARIE-LOUISE."

          "Laeken, Sept. 29, at 9¼ in the morning.

" MY DEAR ONE,
      " I was awakened by your charming letter of the 28th in which you inform me that you are well. I am very sorry to learn your departure from Flushing is still postponed. This deprives me of the pleasure of seeing you for a day. I do not know why, but yesterday I expected all day to receive an order to rejoin you. You should have seen what a dismal countenance I displayed in the Salon, for whenever the door was opened I expected to see the welcome messenger arrive, but all my hopes were in vain. I assure you that if you delay much longer, I shall not

be able to sleep for impatience. I hope you will not
think I am angry with Princess Pauline ; I pity her
for her sufferings as much as you do, and the only
reason I told you the whole story of the other day,
was the fear that some one might prime you with a
tale against me. I am very well. Yesterday I spent
the evening at home. We are always on the watch
to receive your orders. I shall also remain at home
this evening. I propose to take a drive in the park
of Brussels. The inhabitants have expressed a lively
desire that I should do so. Adieu, my dear, I hope
this may be the last letter I shall write to you, and
that to-morrow I may embrace you in person.
     " Your faithful and tender wife,
                              " MARIE-LOUISE."

Finally :

               " Laeken, Sept. 30, at 7½ in the morning.
     " A few moments ago I received your letter which
has overwhelmed me with joy. I shall start at noon
precisely and hope to be near you at four o'clock.
The Queen of Naples has not yet arrived. I am very
well and await with vast impatience the moment when
I may embrace you in person.
     " Your faithful and devoted wife,
                              " MARIE-LOUISE."

In accordance with her programme, the Empress
arrived at four o'clock. The correspondence therefore
ceased.
     It would be difficult to have any fuller revelation
of Marie-Louise than is given in these letters. We
must, however, add to them one that she wrote from

Antwerp on October 2, to Mme. de Luçay, Mistress of the Robes.

" I have not been able up to the present to carry out the promise I made of writing to you and giving you news of myself. I hope your health is as good as mine. I was not the least fatigued by my journey from Compiègne to Brussels, although I was twenty-two hours in the carriage. Since then *fêtes* and receptions have occupied all my time. I remained ten days at Laeken in the midst of terrific storms and rain, so was only able to go out twice for an excursion in the charming environs. I rejoined the Emperor at Antwerp the day before yesterday. You can easily imagine my happiness. He is in the enjoyment of excellent health. Yesterday and to-day I spent in viewing the dockyards, dykes, and basins constructed by the Emperor. I expect to leave to-morrow at ten o'clock for Breda. There will be only fourteen leagues to travel, but the roads are said to be so dangerous and the horses so bad that over twelve hours will be necessary to make this little journey. I beg you to send me three dresses for the autumn to Amsterdam, as soon as possible, one blue, one pink, one white. I hope to hear in your next letter that M. de Luçay is in better health, and that I shall soon have the pleasure of assuring you by word of mouth of the friendship with which I sign myself,

"Your very affectionate

" MARIE-LOUISE."

This shows how much credence may be placed in the report so carefully recorded by the Queen of Westphalia : " The King has received news from Paris.

They say all is not well between the royal couple, that the Empress is very jealous, and is inexcusably wrong in her attitude to the Emperor. . . . The Emperor, they say, has been furious at this want of deference. The Empress nevertheless has followed the Emperor."

The Empress left Laeken on September 30 after a visit disturbed, not by jealousy, but by a tempest and terrible rain which only allowed her two excursions. After four hours, accompanied only by six post-carriages, she arrived at Antwerp and alighted at the house of the Mayor, M. Cornelissen, where the Emperor had been in residence since one in the morning ; on the evening of her arrival she received the ladies. On October 1, their Majesties went in great state to Nôtre-Dame. The Empress was in full dress in a gorgeous State carriage lined with grey satin, harnessed with eight dapple grey horses, plumed and magnificently caparisoned. Their Majesties were received outside the church door by M. de Pradt, Archbishop of Malines, who discoursed on the virtues of the two Maries. Then followed reviews and the launching of ships, a full programme. On October 4, at 2 a.m., the Emperor set out to inspect the coast. The Empress did not leave Antwerp until ten o'clock. She slept at Breda and reached Gorcum for dinner, where the Emperor had been awaiting her for two hours. Next day the horses were ordered for eight o'clock ; the Empress was not ready until ten, consequently they arrived at Utrecht at three o'clock instead of at noon. They stayed at the Palais Impérial, formerly the Royal, which Louis had entirely refitted for a residence that

K

lasted only two months in all. There were three days
of reviews, receptions, and audiences. Their Majesties
did not appear at the ball given by the city. At
Utrecht, Marie-Louise purchased two cases of toys :
not to be opened before her return. Such was the
souvenir she kept from Utrecht.

Their Majesties departed for Amsterdam between
nine and ten in the morning. The travelling carriages
halted outside the gates ; the Empress entered the
State coach, and the Emperor mounted his horse to
ride in the military procession, which comprised four
regiments of cuirassiers, the whole of the cavalry, with
a guard of innumerable foot-soldiers lining the route.
The usual receptions, audiences, Masses, presentations,
and theatrical performances followed. None of the
Dutch were invited to the reception, only the travelling suite being admitted. While the Emperor was
away from her in the Island of Texel for three days
inspecting the fleet, Marie-Louise explored the shops
to such good effect that she exhausted her purse. She
wrote : " I greatly fear the Emperor will think it wrong
of me to ask him for an extra subsidy for my toilet, so
I shall wait for a day when he is in a very good temper
to speak to him about it." She had, indeed, made
large purchases, " linen finer than cambric to be used
for nightdresses, and many other goods of which the
name and country are a secret. I am bringing you
back teapots of Boucaron (Bokhara) and some old
Chinese lacquer which I picked up myself in the best
shop in Amsterdam." This she preferred to running
about the environs, however pretty they might be, for

she remarked, " One sees so much water here, that one is soon disgusted with it."

On the Emperor's return a *fête* with its full accompaniment of flowers and quadrilles was held as at the Tuileries. There were performances at the Théâtre Hollandais in which Mme. Watier, the great Dutch tragedian, took part, representations displaying the skill of the French actors, Talma, Duchesnois, Bourgoin, and Dumas. On the 24th they left for Leyden, The Hague, Rotterdam, Gouda, and the Loo. Marie-Louise had only one idea, to get away from the bad climate of Holland. The Emperor, too, seemed in haste to be off. On the 30th they were at Niméguen, and after an adventure at the Château of Ottenberg, where they were obliged to stop without either sleeping accommodation or supper, the Empress arrived at Dusseldorf, where she was lodged at the Château de la Venerie. Presentations were made, and *fêtes* and excursions organised, about which Roederer, Minister of State, and Beugnot, Minister of the Grand Duchy, were most enthusiastic, having described them as " The prettiest of the whole journey, not excepting Amsterdam ; but the Empress is satiated with *fêtes* and is half dead with fatigue." At cards she answered the Emperor in monosyllables, the others by monotonous movements of her head. This whirl of travel was not yet at an end.

On the 4th, owing to despatches from Paris, the Emperor decided on an immediate return. At Cologne he would hardly allow the Empress twelve hours in which to adore the famous relics and inspect the treasures. The journey had to be rushed through in three days. On account of Marie-Louise, halts were made for lunch and at night ; from Cologne they went to Liège, from Liège to Gurt, but the Marne, owing to flood, had carried away the bridge of boats ; it was not until midday that they were able to cross, by a flying bridge constructed by the English prisoners at the depôt ; they were forced to sleep at Mézières, which they left on the 10th at six in the morning, and breakfasted at Rethel. From there they passed through Rheims, and at ten at night arrived at Compiègne. Next day at seven in the evening they reached Saint-Cloud. At the entrance of the Grand Vestibule the Empress found her son in the arms of his governess. She wrote : " You were quite right to say how delighted I would be to see my son again after a journey of two months ! What I felt in my heart it is impossible to express in words."

That ended the travels for this year. Their Majesties remained three weeks at Saint-Cloud, and then returned to Paris for the 1st of December.

CHAPTER VII

THE days passed. Many entertainments were given, including balls, plays, and quadrilles, in reality plays in which the princesses and the ladies of the Court were the actresses. The Quadrille of the Queen of Naples and that of Queen Hortense, the one in honour of the King of Rome, the other for le Roi Soleil, were both performances with which to amuse the gallery. Great events were looming on the horizon.

Already, during their visit to Amsterdam, mis-understandings had arisen between France and Russia, and Napoleon had shown in many ways that his sentiments towards Russia were not very cordial ; for instance, he took very little interest in Zaandam, famous as the temporary abode of Peter the Great, also he removed the bust of Alexander from Marie-Louise's piano. The movements of the troops showed hostilities were premeditated ; the Emperor, however, imagined he could still conceal his hand. He devised a scheme to involve his father-in-law in the dispute, thinking perhaps that by showing how close was the alliance between the two Empires, he might prevent the war. He wished, therefore, to meet the Emperor before setting out to take command of his armies.

The Emperor came as far as Dresden, so spared his son-in-law half the journey.*

Napoleon left Saint-Cloud on May 9 at half-past five in the morning ; Marie-Louise was in his carriage, and the suite was even more numerous and more brilliant than that which attended their Majesties on the journey to Holland. There was no military escort for the Emperor (all the military forces having been at Posen since the beginning of May), but thirty-nine honorary officers accompanied him and seventeen waited on the Empress. As for the paid retinue, the chamber, table, pantry, kitchen, and livery services were even better equipped than in the earlier journeys through the Empire. At Dresden, the Emperor Napoleon (although the guest of the King of Saxony) would receive the King of Saxony and the Emperor of Austria ; and (with the exception of the State carriages which were to be provided by the West-phalian Court and the Saxon Court) everything would be French, and the whole ceremony was to be carried out in the French manner.

" The Emperor has left to-day to proceed to the inspection of the Grande Armée assembled on the Vistula," one may read in Le Moniteur of the 9th. "H.M. the Empress will accompany His Majesty as far as Dresden, where she hopes to have the pleasure

---

* I may be permitted here to refer to the valuable documents which I published in the numbers for March-April and May-June, 1914, of La Révue des Etudes Napoléoniennes on Le Rôle de l'Austriche en 1813, despatches from M. de Lebzeltern to Metternich. The complicity of Austria with Russia from the month of March, 1812, is established by the text of these despatches.—F. M.

of meeting her august family. She will return at the latest in July."

Although they were to travel incognito as far as Mayence, at Châlons the Emperor received the authorities after dinner, and their Majesties spent the night at the Préfecture. On the 10th at Metz, where they also stayed the night, the Emperor visited the Arsenal, reviewed the troops, and assured himself that the fortifications were in good order. They started for Mayence at half-past two on the morning of the 11th and arrived there during the day. This was the first appearance there of the Empress. Their Majesties were lodged in the Palais de l'Ordre Teutonique, notwithstanding the Artillery School was established in it ; nevertheless it was turned out by order of the Emperor, and the Palace was converted into the Imperial Head-quarters. The Grand Duke and the Grand Duchess of Hesse-Darmstadt came to pay their respects, together with the Hereditary Prince and a number of the Princes of the Rhine. Their Majesties remained over the 12th for reviews, receptions, and audiences. On the 13th they breakfasted at Aschaffenburg as guests of the Prince Primate and dined and slept at Wurtzburg under the roof of the Grand Duke, uncle to Marie-Louise. Here they met the King of Wurtemburg and the Grand Duke of Baden. Everywhere they were welcomed with salutes of cannon, troops, the ringing of bells, and illuminations ; but from Mayence onwards the escorts were provided by the Cavalry of the Guard, only at the frontier of Saxony did the Emperor, after receiving the congratulations of the Saxon Grand Chamberlain, accept an escort of the Saxon Guards. They slept at Plauen, and reached Freyberg on the 16th, where they dined. They were received by the King and Queen of Saxony with whom they entered Dresden at half-past eleven at night. The Emperor had declined the offer of the Saxon State coaches ; nevertheless the city was illuminated, all the troops were under arms, while the cannon thundered, the bells pealed, and at the Palace, the Royal family with the whole Court awaited the Emperor, to conduct him to the suite of apartments called after Augustus II., which had been reserved for him.

The Empress wrote on the 17th to Mme. de Luçay : " I write to you from my bed to let you know we arrived at Dresden safely yesterday at half-past eleven in the evening. The Emperor is well. I am excessively fatigued by the heat and the bad roads."

The Empress made no public appearance, but dined tête-à-tête with the Emperor. On the following day at midday the Emperor and Empress of Austria arrived. Marie-Louise, who had been forbidden to meet her father, wrote to excuse herself and to express how very excited she would be until the moment arrived when she could reassure him of her filial affection.

The reigning Empress of Austria was Maria-Ludovica d'Este, a pretty little woman, with wicked eyes, who from birth had dreamt of war against the French and brought to bear on it the love of intrigue which she had inherited from her maternal ancestors. Her mother, Maria-Beatrix-Ricarda, was the daughter of the Duke of Modena and of Maria-Teresa Cibo Malaspina, Princess of Massa and Carrara. She had been forced to marry an Arch-Duke, and from their union sprang the house of Este-Modena, who upheld the traditions of violent hatred of France and the leaders of the Revolution. From her very first interview with Napoleon, Maria-Ludovica could scarcely conceal her dislike. She wrote to her mother complaining of the way in which Napoleon had all but embraced her and had actually kissed her, while he fired off a volley of questions to which she was careful not to reply ; also expressing her resentment because Marie-Louise had come into her rooms in full toilette covered with diamonds.

Marie-Louise also was out for revenge. She was very indignant that her mother's place had been filled so quickly by this Princess whose reputation was by no means unblemished ; she had watched the new Empress precipitate Austria (hardly yet recovered from the defeats of 1805) into a fresh war in which it had all but perished, while Marie-Louise herself had been sacrificed as surety for peace. Even in her travelling over the country as one of the exiled, she had been the victim of Maria-Ludovica. It was only right she should now take her revenge. She had singularly improved in looks, until her appearance now was so elegant people hardly recognised her. Her figure was charming, her little feet ravishing, added to which every one was talking of her suite,

her hundred and fifty valets de chambre, pages, and
lackeys. The Emperor of Austria himself had but
two. Maria-Ludovica (who in order to avoid rivalry
and comparison of ornaments, had adopted the
Hungarian costume which suited her to perfection)
passed her time rummaging through her step-
daughter's belongings and never emerged empty-
handed. Napoleon, convinced that Maria-Ludovica
would at length yield either to his blandishments or
his power, exerted himself to please her and to win
her favour. "He believes he has conquered her,"
remarked his secretary. In a few days she capitulated
to the ascendancy which he exerted over every one.
Napoleon passing through the apartments, with his
hat in one hand, while the other rested on the door
of the Empress's Sedan chair, talked to her gaily and
adopted airs of intimacy. The Empress appeared to
be deeply interested in his conversation, for she
listened, and answered him with eager interest.
Napoleon was convinced she felt specially attracted
to him when she was with him, and remarked, "Her
face was agreeable and piquante, with something
quite characteristic about it." She was 'a very
pretty little nun.' She let him think what he liked,
so with the fatuity of the man who with money in
his hand had never failed to soften the heart of a
fair, cruel lady, he instantly imagined he had won
her and allowed himself to be hoodwinked. Naturally
she won *him*. Hers was the decisive throw. She
had anticipated the influence the son-in-law would
acquire over the father-in-law, if given a free hand,

and she intended to remain the undisputed mistress
of the husband who was in her toils.

It was not enough for Napoleon that the Emperor
Francis had handed over to him the Austrian army to
use as he wished ; but he had decided that Francis
himself should take command, should enter Russia,
and personally take part in the campaign ; and
moreover, take part with him. That would indeed
have been in direct opposition to the arrangements
that Lebzeltern had made with Russia; but Maria-
Ludovica was on the watch. She used all the means
in her power, reproaches, prayers, and tears, to
prevent her husband engaging in this adventure
which would have linked his policy for ever with that
of France. As a final expedient, although not having
any confidence in Metternich, who, she believed, had
been won over to the French by handsome bribes, she
nevertheless appealed to him for support, and to her
surprise he supported her. The Emperor Francis
declined to set out ; he resisted the influence his
son-in-law brought to bear on him, and yielded to
the representations of his wife and Metternich. The
snare was laid ; if Russia would play her part, Austria
would be ready to finish off the foe.

This drama was enacted amid the most sumptuous
fêtes. The table was laid for sixteen princes, sometimes in the apartments of the Queen of Saxony, where
the superior officers of the Saxon Court acted as
attendants, sometimes in the apartments of the Emperor of France. The _levée_ was usually held in the
quarters of the Emperor of France, occasionally in

those of the King of Saxony. Now and then dinner
was followed by a concert. They hunted one day ;
the princes on horseback, the princesses in carriages ;
two boars were killed. On the 26th the King of
Prussia arrived from Dresden and the Emperor paid
him a formal call. He was then invited with his son,
the Prince Royal, to dine with the King of Saxony,
and a banquet took place on the 27th in the great
dining-hall, served by the pages of Saxony assisted
by the officers of the chamber.

On the 28th, the Fête-Dieu, Marie-Louise attended
the Mass celebrated by the Archbishop of Malines ;
the Emperor at three o'clock bade farewell to the
Emperor of Austria, the Grand Duke of Wurtzburg,
the Prussians, Saxons, and the Princess Augusta.
The entire Court attended the Emperor's dinner as
he was to depart at three in the morning. Marie-
Louise's tears must have convinced the most in-
credulous that she loved her husband very sincerely.
The Emperor himself seemed preoccupied. He always had been anxious in Josephine's time at the
opening of a fresh campaign, and on this occasion,
had he not cause for uneasiness ? His departure
was delayed beyond the appointed hour, and his
agitation was shown by his incessant pacing to and
fro between his apartment and that of the Empress.

The carriages only rolled off at half-past four in the
morning. " You know me sufficiently well," wrote
Marie-Louise to Mme. de Luçay, " to understand
how sad and unhappy I am. I try to control myself,
but I shall be like this until I see him again." In

this state she was more than ever in need of demonstrative affection and tender caresses, therefore she gladly arranged to go to Prague for six weeks, where her sisters and brother, her uncle, and the whole of her family might visit her.

The Austrians left Dresden on the morning of the 29th. Marie-Louise, who was to be received as Empress, prolonged her stay in Dresden, where the Saxon family, the Queen of Westphalia, and the Grand Duke of Wurtzburg lavished attentions on her ; her uncle himself was to accompany her to Prague. On June 4, at five in the morning, she left Dresden with an escort of Saxon Cuirassiers ; she was received in Bohemia with Imperial honours.

At Teplitz she made a point of promenading at the baths as was the habit of every fine lady in Europe ; she slept there, and departed again next day at seven in the morning. Their Austrian Majesties met her at the Abbey of St. Margaret, which she reached at four o'clock, and seated herself on the right of her stepmother's carriage. On the 6th she entertained her father and stepmother at dinner in her apartments, and sat in the centre of one of the long sides of the oval table, with the Préfet du Palais standing opposite her, having the Emperor on her right hand with the Empress on her left. This was her usual procedure, as is shown by the following : "Her Majesty the Empress of France generally occupied the centre place, whether in her own apartments or in those of their Austrian Majesties, or at the play."

It was a difficult matter to keep the peace between the Austrian household and her French household. The universal detestation of France made the Austrians extremely uncordial to the Court of the Tuileries. Already at Dresden, this attitude of coldness and rumour had been displayed by the Empress of Austria's ladies. It must be admitted that Marie-Louise placed herself at the head of the French faction, but this was only natural seeing that the influence of her lady-in-waiting was paramount with her. She wrote to Mme. de Luçay : " I assure you that, in spite of my old gowns, your self-respect as mistress of the robes need not be wounded, for they are thought splendid, and really are marvellously effective amid all the frumpish toilettes that one sees here." She affected only to like and esteem what was French, and on all occasions paraded her love for the Emperor. She wrote : " He is wonderfully well and always gives me the hope of seeing him shortly, God grant this may be true ! I should be too unhappy but for this. They entertain me with perpetual *fêtes* which only make me sadder. My uncles come to visit me. I could be perfectly contented here if the Emperor were with me, but without him, there is no happiness for me."

At Prague every day at least one Arch-Duke came to see this sorrowful lady who, in spite of everything, looked remarkably well. She walked daily in the gardens and visited the Bubenetz Park, Prince Matislau, Count Clam, Count Chotek ; she also attended balls, and plays in Czech, such as *The Siege of Prague by the Swedes* or *Bohemian Loyalty and Courage.* No pains were spared to find congenial amusements for the Empress ; her favourite diversion was riding with her father who had made her a present of the horse she rode. The Empress in her turn lavished on every one tokens of her generosity ; she sent to Paris for flowering bulbs, bracelets, boxes of preserved fruits, "trinkets containing a horse, three saddles and all the fittings of the harness," tables with thirty-six games purchased at the *Singe Vert ;* she exerted herself to find out what her friends required, and presented them with all the most elegant Parisian novelties. For instance, she commissioned Biennais to send a dressing-case costing 26,000 frs., with others at 1500, 1200, and 1000 frs., also an inkstand at 13,000 frs. ; from Mugnier, two gold watches at 1500 frs. ; from Corbie and Gabriel, nine cashmere shawls at prices ranging from 3250 to 1800 frs. ; she ordered from the drapers thirty-nine piece robes, twenty-five gowns from Leroy, fifteen of which were for her stepmother ; Despaux provided thirty-two hats ; Corot, Guérin, and Vaulont every imaginable kind of trimming in artificial flowers ; Tessier twenty-four pairs of stockings at anything from 96 frs. to 72 frs. the pair ; she ordered twenty-two fans in all the fashions then made in Paris ; a drawing-room suite, chairs and arm-chairs ; chenilles for embroidering with gold and silver-gilt shuttles ; twelve dozen pairs of gloves ; a mahogany bookcase enclosing a hundred and forty-nine volumes bound in green morocco with armorial bearings for which special dies were engraved. She exerted her ingenuity to find corsets, toys, bonbons, and chocolate ; in fact, Paris was ransacked for her presents. Her total expenditure amounted to 122,642 frs. 70 c., of which the main portion was for Maria-Ludovica. The latter, however, missed no opportunity of showing her hostility to France and her step-daughter, and there was great difficulty in averting an open rupture.

The French suite were exhausted by their stay in Prague. The long dinners, tedious receptions, glittering illuminations, endless concerts, excursions in carriages and the strenuous attendance in the salons, which required a serious demeanour, with at the same time a keen watchfulness against any infringement of prerogative. " That is approximately what these much coveted pleasures amount to." So said one who had much wished to be of the company.

The visit to Prague lasted a whole month, and the return was fixed for the beginning of July. Most of the Arch-Dukes had already departed, but audiences still had to be given to the entire Austrian Court. Napoleon admitted having satiated every one who approached him with diamonds. The presents from Marie-Louise were not less valuable. Most of them appeared under the 125,000 frs. charged in the Grand Chamberlain's account ; in addition she had emptied her own purse. " I have nothing left for private expenses," she wrote to Mme. de Luçay. " I have been obliged to give away a great deal in Prague, but shall economise next month so as not to be in arrears."

On July 1, at seven in the morning, Marie-Louise

departed with her father; her stepmother and her sisters accompanied her to the carriage, and the procession set out amid the ringing of bells, while troops lined the route. It rained all day, and they were obliged to postpone their visit to the gardens of Count Czernin at the Schönhof. They slept at Carlsbad, where they halted to look at the curiosities, and on the 4th, at Schönfeld they descended the tin mines; on the 5th the night was spent at Franzbrünn near Egra, where, on the morning of the 6th, the Emperor took leave of his daughter. By midnight of the same day, after travelling over shocking roads, Marie-Louise reached Bamberg, where the Duke of Bavaria, Berthier's father-in-law, paid his respects to her. The Duke, surrounded by all the members of the Bavarian Government, had been waiting at the foot of the staircase of his palace (that tragic palace) since six in the evening, the hour appointed, but at one in the morning he had the honour of dining with her Majesty. On the 7th, Marie-Louise was at Wurtzburg, where she found her uncle who had been her devoted companion from Dresden, and had only preceded her for the final preparations. Marie-Louise remained with him a whole week, which passed off very happily. She spent her time in sylvan excursions, picnics, and concerts in which the Grand Duke exhibited all his talents as " Cantor of the Cathedral."

Marie-Louise, however, was full of fancies, as her letter of July 9 shows. "My health is very good notwithstanding a sharp pain in the stomach yesterday." Again on the 10th: "I have great pain in

L

one arm, and am packed up in plasters which do not sweeten the air of my room." The plasters must have been efficacious, for on the same day she went riding, held a reception, and was present at two acts of *Le Mariage de Figaro*. On the 14th she decided to leave, and travelled in one day from Wurtzburg to Mayence. On the 15th she left Mayence, travelling day and night, and arrived at five in the morning at the Château de Pange, where M. de Pange, her Chamberlain entertained her with the most lavish and well-arranged hospitality. On the 17th she passed through Metz and slept at Châlons. On the 18th, at seven in the evening, the cannon of the Invalides announced to the Parisians that the Empress had returned to Saint-Cloud.

From May 9 to July 18, two whole months ! Can we say that any one noticed her absence ?

CHAPTER VIII

THE existence led by the Empress from July 18th, the day of her return, to December 18th, when the Emperor arrived unexpectedly, was the most monotonous and uneventful conceivable. She was very lonely, almost entirely *tête-à-tête* with Madame de Montebello and M. Corvisart ; everything relating to ceremonial bored her, so that even when convened by the Grand Chamberlain the Grand Officers were not sure of a reception. Thus, on the 19th, when they presented themselves to offer congratulations on the journey, the Empress pleaded fatigue and refused to receive any one. Nevertheless, according to the orders left by the Emperor, the Empress usually attended the theatre in state on Thursdays, and on Sundays Mass, followed by a reception and diplomatic audience ; on these occasions she did her best, but with little success. She endeavoured, on August 15th, to carry out the programme planned by the Emperor, an account of which was given him each day. As the receptions became more restricted and less frequented, she felt more at ease, for the same faces reappeared each time and she became familiar with these people. " She does the honours with much grace and simplicity. She plays billiards with the persons she selects, . . . and the evening terminates with a concert or a play." When still fewer people came, some of them were astonished at her singular taste for coarseness in conversation, but this was quite usual in the intimate circle of Madame de Montebello.

Despite the attacks of fever, of which she had at least one every three days, and which she could only shake off by distracting herself with long expeditions in the woods of Saint-Cloud, or it may be in consequence thereof, she constantly thought of the Emperor. Without doubting his success, she felt his absence, and in order to afford herself some distraction, she had bracelets made, which she could wear constantly on her arms inscribed with such names and dates as were connected with the most important periods in her life. It was not easy to decipher this enigma in coloured stones, but it ran as follows :

Natrolite	Malachite
Amethyst	Amethyst
Peridot	Ruby
Opal	Iris
Lapis	Emerald
Emerald	**12**
Onyx	Diamond
Natrolite	Emerald
15	Chrysoprase
Agate	Emerald
Opal	Malachite
Uranium	Beryl
Turquoise	Ruby
1769 in small brilliants	Emerald
	1791

27 Malachite-Amethyst-Ruby-Serpentine.
2 Amethyst-Vermeil (coral)-Ruby-Iris-Labrador, **1810.**

This reads: Napoleon, 15 Août, 1769. Marie, 12 Decembre, 1791. 27 Mars, 2 Avril, 1810.

So she occupied herself, ignoring everything concerning France, even when disaster was threatened.

On the day when, in a fit of delirium, the beforementioned General Malet escaped from the Maison de Santé, in which he was confined, to the Place Vendôme, it was described to her as " An outbreak of brigands which was immediately put down," which had occurred during the night in Paris. She took no notice, but remarked to Cambacérès : " What could they have done to me ? " to which he did not reply. She sought distraction at a party at Saint-Leu and another at Maisons, after which she visited the Salon. She wrote : " I am not at all alarmed by the trouble incited by a handful of lunatics (*têtes folles*), for I know too well the good disposition of the people and their devotion to the Emperor." She attended the theatre, where Savary filled up a few boxes and seated some of his people in the audience to provide sufficient enthusiasm. In time even her retinue became slack, and found excuses for absenting themselves, until eventually, out of her whole suite, one single lady only remained. As for the gentlemen, " Their habit was to gamble from morning to night in the *Salon de service*, and the single lady-in-waiting was fortunate if they did not propose she should amuse herself for a while at *trente-et-quarante.*"

Nevertheless, the winter sojourn at Saint-Cloud was a penance. On December 17th the *Moniteur* published the twenty-ninth bulletin which exploded silently, but its effects disintegrated everything. The edifice was shaken, every one anticipated its fall. On the 18th, at half-past eleven in the evening, as the Empress had just gone to bed, and the " red " lady-in-waiting * was about to close the doors and retire, she heard a noise in the adjacent salon. Naturally, after the episode of Malet she imagined assassins. At the same moment the door opened and two men enveloped in fur pelisses deliberately entered. Mdlle. Katzener shrieking, rushed forward, endeavouring to bar the entrance to the bed-chamber ; but one of the men threw aside his cloak and revealed—the Emperor !

The Austrian Alliance, since 1810, had been the primary consideration of the Emperor's *régime,* for he trusted implicitly the piety and honour of his father-in-law. " I hold him in profound esteem," were his very words. Having then such an idea of the family he could hardly feel he had been deceived, or that in giving him his beloved daughter to wife, an Emperor, and this Emperor in particular, should

---

* The six principal ladies (*premières-femmes*) who attended the Empress were known as the *femmes rouges* from the colour of their costume.   Next in rank came the *femmes noires* or wardrobe-women, so-called from their black silk aprons ; below them again the *femmes blanches,* or wardrobe-maids, with white aprons.—*L'Impératrice Marie Louise,* pp. 196 and 203.

have consciously endeavoured to draw him into the abyss. Napoleon never doubted that Austria desired a general peace and claimed to intervene ; he recognised this and indeed desired it, but the question was whether Austria was working in favour of France and in her interests. He undoubtedly recognised Austria's claim to mediate in the ostensible dispatch from Metternich to the Austrian Chargé d'Affaires in Paris (December 9, 1812), but he read : " The blood relations that unite the two Imperial Houses of Austria and France lend a particular character to all overtures made by our august Master. . . . The Emperor of the French appears to have anticipated what is happening at this moment, in so frequently observing to me that the marriage had changed the face of things in Europe," and the Emperor Francis himself intervened to say, " The moment has come when I can prove to the Emperor of the French who I am." Yes, indeed !

On December 30, 1812, also on January 20, 1813, he repeated his assurances, either personally or through his Minister : this convinced Napoleon that the Emperor of Austria was playing his game, that the combinations were settled, and that his father-in-law could not abandon him without dishonouring and disgracing himself. What use would there be in disquieting his wife with the propositions made to the Court of Austria by certain persons he had been acquainted with in Dresden and in Prague ? What was the good of telling her that her stepmother " Favours exclusively all the enemies of the existing

system, and that her society is composed of the most
ardent and most intrepid coalitionists " ?   What was
the good of revealing to her that Maria-Ludovica, as
also her brother Maximilian, had been initiated into
the *Secte des Amis de la Liberté?*   Far better to keep
up appearances by lavishing beautiful garments on
la petite réligieuse. At her step-daughter's expense
the latter accepted, in January, 1813, 1024 frs.
worth of dresses from Leroy ; in February, 2445 frs.
50 c. worth ; in March, 1937 frs. worth ; in May,
743 frs. worth ; in June, 1025 frs. worth.   Later
on there would be blood upon the garments !

As to the Emperor of Austria, in each letter written
to him by his daughter, she repeated the sentiments
of his son-in-law. The Emperor Francis proclaimed
his intention of being represented, at the approaching
Coronation of the Empress, by Prince Esterhazy,
" The most important man of his Court owing to his
wealth and the extent of his possessions." At the
same time he would send Schwarzenberg to Paris,
" To give Europe striking proof of the intentions of
the Court of Austria, by causing the Commandant of
the Auxiliary Corps to make his appearance at the
Court of France, so as to be near his Chief and able
to take orders from him."

Such was the outlook which, though it may have
been deceptive, could hardly remain so for more than
a few days longer. Was it not possible that the
Emperor, in a game of war, had sufficient advantage
to give pause to this Austria, if she became treacher-
ous ? At any rate he decided not to disturb the

Empress ; but left her so confident that when, in mid-June, she heard of Metternich's mission to Dresden, she saw in it only the definite consolidation of the Alliance, and wrote thus to her father : " I may tell the truth to you, namely, that no tidings have given me such pleasure as these, because they have put an end to all my fears and anxieties. In this I recognise your goodness, I am extremely touched by it, and I cannot sufficiently express all my gratitude to you."

As for the Emperor, he could not believe the treachery, but said to Bubna on May 16, " I have held my father-in-law in great esteem ever since I have known him, he arranged this marriage with me in the noblest manner possible. I am most sincerely grateful to him, but had the Emperor of Austria wished to change his policy, he would have been wiser not to encourage an alliance which I am now obliged to regret." On June 26 he received Metternich at Dresden, and the scoundrel whom he had gorged (but of whose appetite he was ignorant) brought him the conditions upon which Austria would consent not to fight against him. These were the renunciation of Illyria, half Italy, Poland, Spain, Holland, the Confederation of the Rhine and Switzerland ; whereupon he exclaimed : " Is it my father-in-law who makes such a project ! It is he who sends you ! How does he wish to make me appear in the eyes of the French people ? " " The Emperor only recognises his duties, and he will fulfil them," replied Metternich. " Whatever fortune may be in store for his daughter, the Emperor Francis is before all else a sovereign and the interest of his subjects will always be his first consideration." "Yes," concluded Napoleon; "what you have said does not surprise me. Everything points to the fact that I have made an unpardonable error. In marrying an Arch-Duchess, I sought to unite the present and the past : Gothic prejudices and the institutions of my era. I have deceived myself, and now realise the extent of my error."

All the mistakes he had perpetrated down to the last, the prolongation of the armistice till August 10, were made on account of his wife, and now, on the eve of facing Europe with the arms on which he felt he could place so little reliance, he wished to see his wife. The Arch-Duchess had been his downfall ; but was the wife responsible ?

On July 16, he addressed a letter from Dresden to Cambacérès, which he calculated should reach Paris on the 20th. On the 22nd it was arranged that the Empress should start in time to reach Mayence on the 24th. The entire journey was planned with minute care. He wrote :

"She will take the Duchess, two Court ladies, two ' red ' women, two ' black ' women, one Préfet du Palais, two chamberlains, two equerries, one of whom will leave twenty-four hours earlier for Metz so as to divide the route ; also four pages will be distributed along the route to reduce the fatigue for these young persons, her *Secrétaire des Commande-ments* if he is well, and her physician, will also accompany her. In addition she will require a Commissariat, so arranged that her table may be well served, for I shall take no one with me, and possibly several kings or German princes may visit her. It will, however, be unnecessary to bring the silver gilt service."

He arranged every detail, the sleeping quarters, the addresses, the post services, the escorts, everything it was possible to foresee. There were eighteen officers and ladies and fifty-one servants. All were in readiness to depart on the night of the 22nd, when a letter arrived from the Emperor enjoining twenty-four hours' delay, which Marie-Louise knew meant war, for her father had just informed her that hostilities were imminent, to which she replied :

" I received your last letter three days ago ; it grieved me very much because I realise the last hope of peace is gone. This thought must be as terrible to you as to me. I pity you inwardly, my dear Papa. I am persuaded that this war will bring many misfortunes. Count upon me, my very dear Papa, and if I can be of any service to you after the issue of events, I shall render it very willingly."

And this is what she wrote in her diary :

" It was on the 23rd of July that I set out upon my journey to Mayence. Never had there been one which was undertaken so gaily, the idea of seeing the Emperor again after three long months of separation enchanted me, but I am much afraid Mme. Montesquiou must have said I had a heart of stone when I took leave of my son without a tear (which does not happen often).

"I left at six in the morning firmly resolved to travel day and night, rather than not arrive at Mayence on the 25th. The road is pretty enough as it winds around Paris; on leaving the Barrière one sees Rincy (le Raincy) on the right, the park is very fine but the house very small. The Emperor once wished to present it to me, but I had the good sense to refuse his offer not wishing to occupy myself with an estate, and was the more pleased afterwards when I learned that it only produced 30,000 frs., and that one is obliged to spend 60,000 frs. annually upon it.

"Next we passed the vast forest of Bondy, which is very beautiful. The road as far as La Ferté-sous-Jouarre, where we lunched, is extremely pretty; many country houses and orchards are to be seen always against a background of hills.

"We breakfasted with the postmaster, who has rather a nice house. The road becomes continually prettier as one approaches Château Thierry, which lies a few leagues further on; the valley narrows until we are surrounded by woods and pretty villages. Château Thierry is rather a badly built little town; the road divides, one branch leads to Châlons and the other to Etoges, the property of the Duchess's father. She spoke to me a good deal about an estate called St. Martin du Bois which is quite near to Etoges and which she wishes to buy to retire to when her services shall be no longer needed.

"When she turns the conversation on to this subject I have the greatest difficulty in the world to prevent myself being angry with her. Nevertheless, it is true that in the delightful society in which we live there is always the uncertainty of the morrow.

The Sovereign who receives you well to-day and treats you as a friend, may exile and forget you to-morrow, therefore, my one prayer is that God will grant that I may never have the heart of a Sovereign. Anyway, at present I feel that if one of my friends were to fall into disgrace to-day he would only be dearer to me.

"Afterwards we passed by the little town of Epernay, which is very pretty ; the Mayor is a wine merchant on a large scale, and has a fine house with conservatories containing exceedingly rare plants. This part of the country is more barren, there are few trees and many fields which have nothing to recommend them. The landscape is monotonous as far as Châlons.

"There were still four leagues before reaching Châlons-sur-Marne, where we arrived at ten in the evening very tired, the waggons and military having cut up the roads. Here I expected to find a good dinner and a good bed, but nothing of the kind.

"The first dinner had apparently fallen into the fire, so they served us one which was not cooked, which consisted of mutton smelling of goat, and roast chickens so called, for I am certain they were old cocks, also eggs which were at least eight to ten days old ; I should have gone to bed fasting had they not brought me some sour cream, which I fell upon, and had an indigestion which called forth some fine lectures from the Chevalier Bourdier, but I do not fear them like those of M. Corvisart.

"I had scarcely got into bed when I heard a horrible noise of big drums and tambourines which had established themselves under my windows, and which, in spite of my entreaties, remained there till one o'clock in the morning. I was lodged at the Préfecture with the Chevalier de Jessaint, who is a very worthy man, but has the misfortune to have a daughter who is out of her mind. There is a pretty garden in front of his windows.

" The town of Châlons is not pretty and has not much commerce.

" On the 24th before leaving, I received the authorities *en passant*, and at six o'clock was in the carriage but without desiring to travel day and night, as the adventures of the previous evening had exhausted me. The country is charming as far as Clermont, where we breakfasted ; there are hills and orchards, fields, and pretty villages.

" On entering the little town of Clermont I was agreeably surprised to meet M. de St. Aulaire, the Préfet, Chamberlain to the Emperor, one of my old acquaintances, who is an excellent man and extremely amiable. He talks wonderfully well, but is a little too pretentious, and I never found myself able to keep up a long conversation with him, but I like to listen to him. I was especially pleased to see him because it was quite a surprise. We conversed together during breakfast at which I also saw the Mayor of Clermont who seems to be a clever young man ; he never forgets to recite a discourse in verse when we pass by this place.

" The environs appeared to be very pretty. They are densely wooded and M. de St. Aulaire told me there were some charming walks. I got into my carriage immediately, and after passing Dombasle we arrived at the descent to Verdun, which is pretty steep, from which one sees Verdun and all the surrounding country, which looks very ugly. Whilst we were passing over the heights, I noticed a number of English, who are recognisable from their appearance and impertinent manner. There was one who attracted our attention, he was holding a very pretty little boy by the hand, who had the most beautiful fair hair.

"There are more than 900 English prisoners, all officers. The little girls presented me with a basket of bonbons while we were changing horses. Verdun is renowned for its sweetmeats. In passing through Maubeuge I made inquiries as to what had become of the little girl whom I had adopted the year before, and whose parents had so shamefully abandoned her to the foster-mother. I was told that as soon as they learned I intended to give her an allowance, they had come to fetch her.

"The road is very ugly till within a league of Metz.

"I admired the fine road that the Emperor had made over the hill; one cannot really take a step without coming across some benefit or great work ordered by the Emperor.

"Half a league along the Moselle one reaches Metz. The city has a melancholy and ancient appearance. Many buildings of which one sees the ruins have been destroyed or burned, and the fortifications do not help to enliven the place. There are from 30,000 to 40,000 inhabitants. I was lodged at the Préfecture in an apartment that the Emperor had occupied last time. We arrived at nine o'clock. After dinner I received the authorities.

"I met again with pleasure the Comte de Pange,

Chamberlain, who is now in the Garde d'Honneur. He has nearly always been in waiting on me since my arrival in France, but is a man of no brilliant qualities, although having much good sense and firmness, and is an excellent man in all respects. I was sorry when he left us because I readily accustom myself to those who are about me when they are worthy, also I dislike new faces, and become attached with difficulty, but when I have a friendship for any one it is for life.

"Prince Aldobrandini made me angry by saying I could not depart next morning before six o'clock. Knowing I had 56 leagues to travel, I was in despair to think I might not arrive until after the Emperor. I attempted to show him the possibility of starting at four o'clock, but he was obstinate, and my resolution, although worthy of a Bretonne, was obliged to yield to his.

"The country as far as Saarbourg where we took breakfast is very pretty with many wooded hills from which there are some lovely prospects. This fine metalled road from Metz which the Emperor made cost much money. Formerly it took more than 60 hours to travel to Mayence through the sand, whereas now, when the surface is good, one can reach it in 17 hours.

"The road, however, was as bad as the weather, it rained in torrents. The distance from Metz to Saarbruck is 17 leagues, through woods and valleys, where there are many foundries and manufactories, especially between Saarbruck, Forbach, Homburg, Bruckruhlbach, and Landsthul as far as Kaiserslautern, a very dirty little town.

"After Saarbruck nothing is spoken but German.

In the background to the left one sees Mount Tonnerre,
which is usually enveloped in clouds. The road leads
through woods of green trees. I prefer these to other
trees, which I think give a melancholy touch to the
landscape.

" We dined at nine in the evening at Kirchen
Boland in a splendid mansion, belonging to a merchant
from Frankfort, who is reported to have an income of
£100,000 per annum. The park must be pretty and
the house is furnished as luxuriously as any of the
largest in Paris. The rain poured incessantly, and
we still had 15 leagues to travel. I lay down as best
I could in the carriage, but we advanced so slowly
that we were still a league from Mayence at four in
the morning. I then saw before me all the mountains
of the Rheingau and the Hunsrucken, and at five
o'clock we entered the first gate of the fortifications
of Mayence. Everybody was tired of waiting for us,
so had gone to bed, and I was much pleased when on
leaving the carriage, General Fouler brought me a
letter in which the Emperor told me he should not
arrive before the day of the 27th. I cast myself at
once upon my bed, but could not sleep.

" I am lodged in the same house and in the same
apartment as during my last visit, but it has been
refurnished and is much improved ; formerly, one
was devoured by bugs. I have a view over the
Bridge of Boats and the mountains of Wiesbaden
and to the right over a mountain named the Meli-
bocus 15 leagues away, upon which there is a Roman
tower. The mills are in front of my windows and
make an insufferable noise. Outside my sitting-room
there is a little terrace where one can walk during the

M

great heat. I spent the whole of the next day at the window watching the Bridge of Boats and the road to Frankfort, for knowing the Emperor must come that way I thought he might very likely surprise me by arriving on the 26th. My watching was in vain, so I went to bed dying of sleep. Every one was so tired that when the Emperor did arrive he came through all the *salons* in which the page and my women slept without any one hearing him. I will not attempt to describe the joy I felt at seeing him again, that cannot be written but only felt. He looked well and in very good spirits.

" I spent the whole morning of the 27th at home and received the authorities. The mayor told me there was scarcely any trade now at Mayence. The city suffered a great deal during the first wars, one can still see bullet marks on all the houses. Since the Emperor's reign, however, the population has increased ; there are now as many as 40,000 in-habitants. The Préfet is an old man, by name M. Jambon St. André.

" In the evening I took a short walk along the road to Frankfort ; this is not a pleasant route as it necessi-tates passing the Bridge of Boats and Fort Cassel (Castel), which is opposite Mayence, and the road thither is detestable. The country is beautiful, one walks in alleys of fruit trees and fields, all the time looking on to the high mountains of the Rheingau.

" We had company to dinner, among whom was Maréchal Kellerman ; the wine made him rather lively, and he insisted that I ought to drink a great deal ; however, he gained my esteem that day because he had the courage to tell the Emperor several times

that he was doing an injustice in not giving the Cross
to an engineer whom he named.   I do not know
whether he always speaks the truth like this, or whether
the wine gave him this frankness.

" On the 28th the heat was still appalling.   In
the morning I received a visit from the old Prince de
Nassau with his wife and the two princesses, his
daughters.   The mother is very witty, but the two
princesses are hideous.   The eldest, who is as fat as
Prince Schwarzenberg, had only been married three
days to a Prince of Baden, when she was divorced
from him because she had an infatuation for one of
her father's grooms ; as for the younger, I hardly
know what to say, for she shows no intelligence, nor
does she utter more than a couple of words during
the day.   Some one who knows this Court told me
that during the six years he had known her he had
never yet heard her voice.   They have another
daughter who is out of her mind, who threw herself
into the Rhine last year, and I am very much afraid
that the little princess will shortly do the same.

" I went in the evening to Wiesbaden Baths which
are three leagues from Mayence.   I followed the same
road as the evening before to a village in another
direction ; in the distance, in an obscure and romantic
valley, can be seen the rock which bears the ruin of
Sonneck, a castle of the Emperor Adolf of Nassau,
in which he hid his mistress and where his hound came
to seek her to lead her to the field of battle on which
his master had perished.   Wiesbaden is at the foot
of the mountains.   A number of new houses are being
built in the town.   The baths, which are beneficial
for wounds and rheumatism, are much frequented,

especially by Poles. The Assembly-room is very fine
and worthy of a large capital; it has a small garden
prettily laid out with a sheet of water. The view on
the return journey is superb. The Rhine, the town
of Mayence, and the Malibocus with its white tower,
lie to the left, while on the right are the mountains
which I intend to explore.

"I found the Emperor at Cassel visiting the fortifications : we embarked upon the Rhine, then had
a beautiful walk while the sun was setting. We
returned by carriage along the right bank of the Rhine,
which is the promenade of the Mayençois.

"After dinner at ten o'clock the Emperor proposed
a walk upon the terrace. In vain I suggested my short
sleeves were not in keeping with the recommendations
of my doctor. He grew angry and called physic and
physicians fools, and I was constrained to obey, which
gave me an attack of rheumatism in the right arm.

"On the morning of the 29th I received the Grand
Duke and Grand Duchess of Hesse-Darmstadt and
her brother. The Grand Duchess must have been
very beautiful; she is fifty years old, and with the aid
of a little rouge and white powder is still handsome ;
though very large and stout she is well made, she
converses well and apparently is clever. The Emperor
has since told me I was quite right, that she was very
clever, and some years ago endeavoured to incite the
Grand Duke against the Emperor, but the latter
perceived it, and compelled the Grand Duke to exile
a young *émigré* who was more than a friend to the
Grand Duchess, who did all she could to get him
back ; the Emperor was inexorable, since when,
fearing a similar fate might await his successor, she

has been charming to the Emperor, and now endeavours
to render him all the services in her power.

"I saw also the Prince of Nassau and the Prince
of Isenbourg. The Emperor fortunately put an end
to all these visits and came to spend the morning with
me as hitherto. I read to him out of *Gil Blas*; he asked
for the part about Doctor Sangrado, which amused
him very much; I laugh at it but only in secret,
having a profound respect for doctors and being far
too frightened of all drugs (especially those of
M. Bourdier) to call down their vengeance upon me.

"I went to see Biberich, the residence of the Duke
of Nassau; it is on the same side as Wiesbaden, on
the bank of the Rhine; the castle is very large but
Gothic. The Prince and his eldest daughter showed
me the garden. They have made the old castle very
pretty and furnished it inside in modern style. They
made me sit upon a couch which was not very comfortable and told me there was a bath underneath, I
rather suspect it was something else! They served
us with sour cream, politeness compelled me to
swallow a mouthful, but the same thing nearly
happened to me as to the painter in *William Pikle*,
when the doctor in the repast *à la romaine* forced him
to eat a hash of glow-worms and asafœtida.

"We had the Grand Duke and Grand Duchess of
Hesse-Darmstadt to dinner; the Emperor lectured me
severely because I was not ready when she arrived.
I dread nothing more than to see the Emperor angry
with me, but would sooner die than give him the
pleasure of witnessing my pain by crying on account
of his reproaches, so I restrain my grief until the
Emperor is out of the room.

" On the 30th, the Grand Duke of Baden and the Prince Primate came to see me in the morning; how tedious these visits are, these demonstrations of friendship for people for whom one does not care are terrible! It must, however, be noticeable in my expression, for on meeting my friends, I am talkative enough to be choked by the words I wish to say, whereas with other people I find the greatest difficulty in the world in framing a single sentence.

" The heat was intense all day; in the evening I made an excursion with the Emperor in a boat. We ascended the Main which flows into the Rhine a short way above the last fortifications; the evening was magnificent, every one was gay except myself, for this was the evening before the departure of the Emperor.

" We had company to dinner. The Prince Primate is very amiable. After dinner he told me some amusing anecdotes more worthy of a lieutenant than of a Prince of the Church. They made every one laugh, but are too droll to be written here.

" The weather was rather uncertain on the 31st. I spent the morning with the Emperor and endeavoured to be cheerful. At eight o'clock I took a little walk in a pretty wood of fir trees on the right bank of the Rhine. The weather became very stormy and we could scarcely see the mountains, which made us foretell bad weather for our voyage upon the Rhine. In the evening the Emperor received a great many people. As it was the eve of his departure, he also had an important discussion with the Prince Primate about the woods of Spessart that the latter wished to sell to him.

" On the 1st, after Mass, the Emperor decided to depart immediately. The equipages could not be ready before four o'clock. I was obliged to attend the dinner to which he had invited all his household, but have now learned to control myself so as to assume a cheerful countenance !

" I endeavoured to be calm until the Emperor entered his carriage as he felt too much grief at parting for me to add to his distress. My courage upon this occasion satisfied me ; however, I might have done better, for I recollect having had a great sorrow some time ago which I disguised so well that the Emperor said to me, ' I do not know you, you are too sprightly to-day.' It took all my pride to deceive him, and I paid dearly for it afterwards, for I suffered for a long time.

" The evening passed very sadly, it is to be hoped that I shall not have many such in my life. I gave orders for my departure next day, it was so lonely at Mayence.

" On the 1st of August, at nine in the morning, I went on board the yacht, which really had the appearance of a small man-of-war ; there were three cabins, a saloon, a bedroom, and a dining-room, besides several other closets. I went up on the deck immediately where a fine awning had been prepared for us. The yacht belongs to the Prince of Nassau, who lent it to me and sent me his Grand Ecuyer, Grand Maréchal, Grand Veneur, Grand Chambellan (the same person holds all these offices) to accompany me. This did not prevent my ladies ridiculing the princesses before him. Their behaviour made me very indignant, only the Duchess refrained, but she is a perfect woman, such as there never was before. The yacht, carried along by the current, travelled fairly fast. We made a league in the hour.

" Mayence receded by degrees, until we passed before Biberich (Biebrich), the castle of which, seen from the Rhine, has an imposing aspect. The two Princes of Nassau came to bid us farewell. Many boats with music, and others with cannon, resounded over the Rhine. I confess I could have done very well without the latter, but the former, in conjunction with the important places which we passed, made our whole cruise so *romanesque* and romantic, it stirred my imagination. My thoughts were carried back to olden times, and pictured the ancient castles, in all their splendour, inhabited by brave lords and fair ladies.

" The condition of women, however, was not as agreeable then as now, for they had often only one room for their family, and to me a fine apartment is one of the pleasures of life.

" Near Biberich are some very pretty islands in the Rhine which is very broad there ; on the left lies a plain, while on the right are high mountains in the distance, with vine-covered hills in the foreground. We passed Walluf where the Rheingau connects, before which is the village of Scheisten (Schierstein) where are the country houses of Count Stadion. Ellfold (Eltville) a pretty little town with an ancient Gothic tower, is upon the same bank.

" Upon the left bank is the fringe of the forests of pine trees which dwindle away in the *landes* near Ingelheim. Near Eltville is the village of Esbarck (Esbach) which contains a Carthusian Monastery half destroyed, lying in a delightful valley in the mountains. We were told it had once been very rich, and the church is said to contain many fine tombs. On the left side we were able to see Tulpheim on a hill in the distance. What recollections this city calls up ! Nothing now remains of its former greatness but a few ruins ! There is not a vestige of the Palace of Charlemagne.

" On the island in the Rhine, Louis le Débonnaire died, and here Henry IV. Emperor of Germany was despoiled of his crown. Here also Emma, during a dark night, bore Eginard upon her shoulders through the snow, to conceal the print of his footsteps from Charlemagne. I think nothing is more interesting than a journey which recalls historical reminiscences.

" Near Hatteheim (Hattenheim) is another splendid view ; the best Rhine wines are grown near Ostreich (Ostrich) and Mittelheim. While passing these places we took breakfast on board the yacht. Here the hill called Johannesberg, which belongs to the Duke of Valmy (it was formerly the demesne of an abbey), is planted with vines from top to bottom, and produces 400,000 frs. worth of excellent wine ; the view from it is said to be magnificent. The Convent of the Nuns, called the Gottesthal, is concealed in an obscure and picturesque valley ; its solitude is supreme, and it is well situated for its purpose, whether as a retreat for meditation, or if one should wish to be alone when in distress. I feel that were I to experience great misfortunes or losses, I would willingly bury myself in this convent.

" We passed by Geissenheim (Geisenheim), a pretty little town ; between it and Rüdesheim there is a magnificent abbey called Enbingen (Eibingen) (now abandoned) situated on a mountain, where they used to show the ring of an Abbess Hildegarde, famed for her prophecies and writings, which bore the motto ' I love to suffer.' This made me feel less virtuous than her, for I should not choose that device.

" At this place the Rhine widens considerably, forming a basin before it plunges into the gorge of Bingen. To the left is the Mountain of St. Roch (Rochusberg) and on the right Rüdesheim with its ruins. On our arrival we found a book on the table, from which we learnt that in the old castle the portraits of the Brömser family are preserved. This family flourished in 938. This was enough to tempt any one even less curious than ourselves, so we resolved unanimously to go and see them. The heat was dreadful and the wind against us, so we were obliged to beat about for an hour before we could reach our destination. We climbed up the mountain courageously and saw the ruins of an old castle, of little importance, built in the time of the Romans, but with no gateway. You may imagine our fury at having been put out of breath for nothing. When we reached the yacht we were told that the portraits were about 300 paces away, but disappointed by our first experience, we contented ourselves with the description and went on another tack.

" We were still an hour from Bingen where we entered the gorge. On the heights are some delightful pleasure gardens belonging to a German Count. The wind became so strong that we were continually driven back, and it was necessary to double the crew to manœuvre the vessel.

" In the meantime I amused myself by telling
General Caffarelly that there were some rocks near
Bingen beneath the surface of the water on which
boats were very easily wrecked. This put him into
such a state that I expected him to suggest walking
the remaining ten leagues. It is true that there are
rocks near Bingen which cause certain eddies, but they
have been blasted and are now much less dangerous.

" A wonderful ghost story, connected with the
Castle of Rüdesheim, is told about a young girl who
threw herself into the Rhine and still appears lament-
ing, but it is too long to write here.

" A convent of Capucins called Nothgottes is here,
containing the horns of the ox of Jean Brömser and
the chains worn by him when prisoner in the Holy
Land. To the left at the place where the Rhine
becomes narrower, one can see the town of Bingen
with the old castle of Ehranfels (Ehrenfels) standing
over it. All the cities on the Rhine seem to be ancient
and badly built, having narrow and dirty streets and
no trade. The left bank belongs to the Emperor, and
the right to the Prince of Nassau-(Weil) Wilbourg,
who was with us in Paris. The Rhine turns suddenly
and breaks against the rocks as far as the spot where
the Nahe flows into it.

" This is one of the most picturesque spots, and
the valley of the Nahe is charming. A delightful
feature is a stone bridge. Near the old Castle of
Kloppe (Klopp) are the ruins of the convent of
Ruppertberg (Ruppertsberg) upon a mountain of the
same name, where Hildegarde wrote her prophecies,
and hollowed out a tomb and a well with her own
hand in 1148. For some distance the difference

between the waters of the Nahe and those of the
Rhine is quite noticeable. The former are yellow,
and the latter of a greenish colour.

" From here one sees the Mouse Tower, built upon
a rock projecting into the river ; legend tells us that
Archbishop Hatto of Mayence was devoured by mice
for having refused to give corn to the poor during a
famine. It is almost destroyed and serves as a light-
house to show the famous rocks which caused the
panic of General Caffarelli.

" The country now begins to have a wild appearance, the plain becomes more confined, and if only
the mountains were more wooded, this landscape
would be extremely beautiful. After the twists and
turns which the Rhine makes here, Asmanshausen
(Assmannshausen) comes into view with numbers of
old castles on the summit of the mountains ; then on
the left are Bautzberg (Vauts-) and Kneiptein
(Konigstein), while on the other side is Falkenberg.
I was told a red wine is grown near Asmanshausen
which has the same flavour as Burgundy.

" I much regretted not being able to stay to make
excursions into all the beautiful valleys of which
one here gets glimpses. They are filled with convents
of nuns, on this side is that of Athensen beneath
the ruins of Sooneck. Upon the left bank are seen
the smiling villages of Dreickshausen and Nieder-
heimbach, to the right is the ruin of Lorch, the frontier
of the Rheingau. This ruin is built upon a mass of
inaccessible rocks, crowned by an ancient castle, of
which it is said that the châtelaine who inhabited it
made a vow not to marry any knight unless he should
ride up on horseback. A dozen broke their necks in

the attempt; there was one, however, who made a
compact with the devil and succeeded. He married the
lady and did so many good deeds that the devil dared
not come to fetch him at the time appointed!

"The mountains become less elevated towards
Steinbach and the ruins of Furstenberg and Stahleck
and Bacharach are seen on the right bank of the
Rhine : it was formerly an Imperial City. Near by
there is an altar in the Rhine which the Romans
dedicated to Bacchus, only to be seen at low water.
The town is dominated by the ancient castle of
Stahleck. The wind here became so strong that our
yacht was turned about at least a dozen times, at the
same time it became excessively cold, so everybody
went below. I remained on deck at the risk of catching a fever, to contemplate the beauties of nature ;
moreover to disobey my doctor delighted me! The
Rhine widens again very much here, and one appears
to be in a sort of lake, in the midst of which is the
square Pfloz (Pfalz) built on a rock, without any
entrance except a trap-door, with little loopholes for
windows. According to the old records, this is where
the Palatine Countesses were obliged to pass the period
of their pregnancy and confinement, in an apartment
consisting of a triangular chamber where one would
not even lodge one's waiting-maid. How miserable
the condition of those poor women must have been
in that age of barbarism! It is not even now very
agreeable but I would not change with our great
grandmothers.

"The town of Caub with its old fortress of Gutenfels
is noticeable on the right, from the windows of which
Gustavus Adolphus gave orders to repel the assault

of the Spaniards. It is said the scenery in the country about a league from Caub is very beautiful. Next comes Oberwesel on the left bank with the ancient ruin of Schönberg, whose founder belonged to the Belmont family. On looking back from here one obtains a beautiful view of Caub and the square tower. The industry of the inhabitants in cultivating their vines on every inch of ground is incredible; they even plant them upon some of the steepest rocks and endeavour to prevent the earth crumbling by means of walls. Here is a rock called Luchy (Lurlei) which is quite imposing in its form, where an echo will repeat seven times.

"Near this place is a bank of sand which is a danger to boatmen who do not understand the navigation of the Rhine. The fishermen make use of it in fishing for salmon, they live in huts, and in this respect are not unlike the Laplanders as described in travels; they presented us with two rather fine fish. It is reported that this bank is connected with the eddy at Bingen and boats which have been lost in the latter have reappeared on the bank. We were very agreeably surprised on suddenly coming in view of St. Goar where we were to sleep, which was reached at half-past eight. We were saluted by the cannon of the old fortress of Rheinfels and Goarshausen which are opposite each other.

"St. Goar is a little town with scarcely 2000 souls. The house I occupied looked over the Rhine, on which the illuminated boats made a pretty effect. My apartment was not sumptuous, consisting as it did of nothing but the four walls.

"My love for the beauties of the scenery of the

Rhine cost me dear; I was desperately ill all night, and in the morning had still sufficient fever to prevent any departure before the middle of the following day, after being in a fine passion with poor Chevalier Bourdier who endeavoured to persuade me to swallow syrup of couch grass, camomile, soothing draughts, and a hundred thousand other things which would have poisoned me. I shall do nothing until we reach Paris, and then shall only follow the advice of the *grand médecin.*

" On the 3rd we had tolerably fine weather for our voyage which was accomplished very pleasantly. We passed by Welmich with its remarkably handsome Gothic tower and old castle called the *Mausthurm (Souris).*

" The rocks are quite bare as far as Hirzenach, where there is a very fine abbey. There are gold and silver mines here and more orchards. The Rhine turns eastward, and above Salzig are the two Castles of Liebenstein and Sternfels (Sternberg) called the Two Brothers, about which a charming tale is told, but as it is a long one, my reclining posture will not permit me to write it.

" There was at Bornhosen (Bornhofen) a convent of Capucins which, until two years ago, was still a celebrated place of pilgrimage; it was founded by Brömser, but had to be suppressed on account of the excesses committed there.

" On the left is the town of Boppert (Boppard) with its ancient towers and walls, which is said to be one of the fifty fortresses built by Germanicus in this part of Germany.

" Above the town at Marienberg there used to be

a convent in which were canonesses. The fine road constructed by the Emperor, after overcoming so many difficulties, traverses this bank. It necessitated the blasting of rocks, the building of stone bridges, and the boring of tunnels, and was only completed a few years ago.

" The Rhine widens again considerably, and one suddenly sees Braubach and the old fortress of Marksburg, situated on the rock which is frequently enveloped in clouds, where the Emperor Henry IV. was received after his own son had refused him hospitality.

" The landscape here is much more pleasing for the mountains recede, which brings Oberlahnstein into sight. To the left one sees the little town of Rhens which has a very curious square tower. Four hundred paces from this town in the shade of some walnut trees was formerly the site of the Königsstuhl, but no traces of it can now be seen. Here, in the early days of Christianity, the Emperor and his Seven Electors held their deliberations, and Emperors were elected or dethroned. It was erected on this spot because the States of the Four Electors of the Rhine joined.

" It made me feel sad to see the destruction of monuments of such ancient grandeur, and the pilot who related this story was unable to restrain his emotion. Not a vestige is left of this ancient monument of the greatness of Germany. Opposite this spot across the river is the ruin of the chapel where the Emperor Wenceslas was dethroned by his electors in 1400.

" The little town of Oberlahnstein is charmingly situated on the other bank ; the ruins of the ancient castle of Kochenfels (? Stolzenfels) can be seen, and a little further on one comes to the mouth of the Lahn. Here we were besieged by a quantity of boats which brought us fruit and flowers, meanwhile being saluted with endless volleys of cannon, truly a most painful ordeal both physically and morally. I suffered much from it.

" When the Duchess is present this reminiscence of unhappy memories must be very trying to her. The Lahn flows into the Rhine between the old castle of Lahneck and Neiderlahnstein, its banks are said to be very picturesque and a good hunting ground for botanists and mineralogists; the mouth of it is only half an hour's distance from that of the Moselle; near the Lahn is a very large island in the Rhine on which is a ruined convent founded in 1143, and occupied by nuns up to the time of the Revolution.

" Having left the convent on our right hand, we passed the village of Horschheim, which has a glorious view. In the distance is a Carthusian Monastery on the left hand, to the right the ruined fortress of Ehrenbreitstein, and in front Coblentz with its very fine old residence of the Elector.

" We arrived at four o'clock. I was lodged in the Préfecture having a pretty outlook into a garden, but being still feverish I hastened to retire to bed. M. Bourdier came to see me and told me that two unfortunate gunners who should have been of my guard had lost, one his arm, the other both wrists in endeavouring to discharge a cannon to celebrate my arrival.

" It is very sad to reflect that no journey takes place without occasioning some such accident, though quite innocently.

N

" The town is fairly large and very pretty, but has no commerce.

" In the evening after dinner I received the authorities. Unfortunately I mentioned to General Caffarelli what I had been told about the two gunners. On reaching home he sent for M. Bourdier, and not only scolded him but treated him in a manner one would not even use towards one's servant. When he had vented his anger, he said to him, ' You see I am hasty but it quickly passes off.' I know very well that had I been M. Bourdier I should not have taken it so patiently. General Caffarelli is incredibly hot-tempered and suspicious, at the same time he is an excellent man, quick and clever, but none the less intolerant. In conversation he must always be right, expecting every one to be of the same opinion as himself, which is not always possible, as sometimes he is mistaken ; moreover, the charm of conversation lies in diversity of opinions !

" On the 4th, at eight in the morning, we set out once more, happy that it was the last day of our voyage. We were growing weary of the beauties of nature and found it very tiresome to remain inactive all day. Once again we looked upon Coblentz and the fortress of Ehrenbreitstein, where on the left stands a little pyramid on a low mound to mark the tomb of Generals Marceau and Hoche.

" Neuendorff, a small village also on the left bank of the river, is the place which supplies Coblentz with vegetables. On the right, in the Island of Nidewith (Niederwerth), is a convent, besides two others at Vallesheim (Wallersheim) and Besselich not more than 100 paces away. On the right bank is the town of

Wallendar, which carries on many industries and has
many factories.

"After passing a number of other villages, the names
of which it would be tedious to repeat, we arrived at
Engers, the summer residence of the Princes of
Nassau-Vilburg, which is beautifully situated. The
house is very large but has no garden. The Prince
has made roads through the woods of the adjacent
mountains in which there is an old château called
Eulgen ; to the left is the village of Visterthurm
(Weissenthurm), famous in history for one of the
most bloody conflicts fought at the beginning of the
Revolution between the French and Germans.

" Upon a mountain on the right bank is Montreaux
(Monrepos), the summer residence of the Princes of
Neuwied, constructed entirely of wood.

" After this one of the finest views in the Rhine
voyage may be seen, a smiling plain framed by
mountains, setting off the Abbey of Romes-dof
(Rommers-dorf). Two of the hills in the distance,
on the left, are said to have formerly been volcanoes,
owing to the amount of lava found there. At the
back is a convent of Capuchins situated on the
lake, which is several leagues in circumference, the
bottom of which has never been found.

" Neuwied, a charming little town, is on the right
bank close to the river. The town is well built.
The castle is small but pleasantly situated having
a pleasure garden bordered by alleys of magnificent
poplars. The reigning Princess is a lady brimming
with wit and sensibility, who was left a widow while
very young, with a number of children whom she has
brought up extremely well. She is also an authoress,

the Templars destroyed in 1200. After passing Ahren-
fels and Ariendorf one sees the rock of Erpeley
(Erpeler), a block of granite 700 feet high. Linz is
close to Dattenberg, Breysig, and Sinzig with the old
castles of Obbusken (?) and Landskron, and here the
Rhine forms a lake which is the frontier of the Prince
of Nassau's states.

" The Ahr joins the Rhine here, and in stormy
weather is said to become very dangerous, causing
many shipwrecks. Half a league from Rheinmagen
(Remagen) is the little town of Unkel, where the river
is also very rocky. From this spot can be seen the
seven mountains (Siebengebirge), far-famed as having
been the principal abode of the ' Invisible Tribunal.'
Formerly each was crowned with a castle ; now only
those of Drachenfels and Stolzenberg are left. The
others were destroyed before the year 1000. There
is still a chapel on the Lowenburg.

The stories told of the Secret Tribunal have
always filled me with peculiar fear. I should not like
to have lived in those times, for this fear is justifiable
when one realises that at times even peaceable
knights are said to have heard a rapping at their
door, on which was posted the following morning an
order to present themselves on such and such a day
at the cross roads, to be judged by the Secret Tribunal. If they did not appear at the third summons
they would either be found assassinated in their beds
or hanging from a tree on the highway, placarded
with the announcement that the Secret Tribunal had
exercised its just vengeance. The members of the
Tribunal always wore black, were disguised with masks,
and never showed themselves by day. They passed

judgment in grottoes or caverns and represented
persons of all classes from the prince to the lowest
order of the people. This dread tribunal lasted from
the year 1000 to 1300 or 1400. I know that whenever
people talk to me about it I have terrible dreams;
this happened to me at Cologne.

"Oberwinter is on the left bank of the Rhine in a
very smiling country where some exceedingly pretty
little valleys lie behind this town.

"Several weeks should be given to this voyage on
the Rhine to examine all the picturesque sites at
leisure.

"Oberwinter is almost at the foot of the Seven
Mountains, and opposite to it there is a wooded hill
on which two faces of wall are all that now remains
of a large castle called Rolandseck.

"Nonnenwerth is another island on the river
resembling a pleasure-ground, and having in the centre
a very fine convent, in which there are still a dozen
nuns who were permitted by the Emperor to remain
there, on condition they do not receive any novices.
We saw them as we passed, dressed in black with
violet *fichus;* they looked very old.

"The inhabitants tell a story about the founda-
tions of this convent which is true and may be read
in the Archives of Cologne. Roland, nephew of
Charlemagne, once lost his way and was obliged to
beg hospitality at the Castle of Drachenfels, whose
lord received him with the utmost cordiality. He
was served by the Baron's daughter, who was beautiful
as the day, and offered him wine and bread. Roland
fell in love with her as soon as he saw her. On leaving,
the following morning, the Baron asked his name, and

Roland gave it with modest blushes, for his courage
and loyalty were made known in song by the people.
The old Baron was pleased at having welcomed such
a guest and begged him to remain another day. A
glance from the youthful Hildegarde persuaded him.
On that day Roland found occasion to tell her of his
love. She was seated under an apple tree wearing
a garland of flowers on her lovely fair hair, meanwhile
playing with the birds. All trembling he told of his
passion while Hildegarde looked down and blushed.
Having kissed her hand he vowed eternal fealty to her.
Next day they parted without words, nor did Hildegarde weep, but was overwhelmed with melancholy.
She climbed the tower to gaze upon him once more,
and when she could no longer see the knight, her tears
flowed fast owing to a dread presentiment which
robbed her of all gaiety. Each day she spent in
prayer, vowing to wear the veil until he returned,
and if he did not, then to retire to a cloister for the
remainder of her life. After this her father's castle
was besieged by a neighbouring Baron ; Hildegarde
hoped that Roland would come to deliver her, but
he came not. Secretly she sent a messenger to him,
who returned with the good news that he was on the
way to rescue her father with a considerable body of
men. Roland, in fact, arrived next day and attacked
the assailants, while old Drachenfels made a *sortie* to
aid him.

"Night came on during the battle, with the result
that it was no longer possible to distinguish between
friend and foe, and Roland had the misfortune with
his own hand to slay the father of Hildegarde. The
enemy fled at every point, and Roland was victorious

at the moment when he perceived the old man before him. The damsel arrived with retainers bearing torches ; she gazed fixedly upon the corpse, then clasping the hand of the knight, she said, ' You have committed no murder, but we must part, I feel that the soul of my father forgives you at this moment. You came to help him, but your hand is stained with his blood and I dare not grant you mine. I can only give it to you before we separate, our love must change to mourning. Heaven has willed it, and even if our hearts suffer we must submit to the decree. After burying my father I shall go to the Island Convent ; if you have courage to be constant until the life eternal, we shall meet in Paradise.' Roland felt all the purity of his mistress' love ; he swore eternal fidelity, after which they parted sadly. Hildegarde became a nun in the convent on the island, and Roland built himself a castle opposite, upon the mountain. He spent whole days at the window gazing upon the convent. At break of day when he heard the bell for matins, he listened to the chanting and fancied he recognised the voice of Hildegarde. When at night he detected a glimmer in some dark cell, he imagined it was his lady praying for him. At the end of two years, on a gloomy autumn morning, as he looked out as usual, he noticed a grave was being dug in the cemetery of the convent. Filled with gloomy foreboding, he dispatched a messenger to the convent, and heard that Hildegarde had departed. He saw her body placed in the grave and listened to the last farewell of the living as they chanted for the dead. The following spring he saw the first flowers spring up over her grave ; the next year he, too, was gone !

" I thought this a charming story. Women are still the same, but men are no longer so constant ! I remained till sunset gazing upon the Seven Mountains as they gradually vanished in the distance.

" Here the Rhine Valley ends, to the right in this smiling plain are the villages of Dollendorf and Cassel, with the Abbey of Siegburg, and to the left Roisdorf, Mahlem, and Plittersdorf. Here was Godesberg with its ancient ruin, the finest I have ever seen.

" I never regretted so much as on that day, that I was not then sufficiently skilled in drawing to be able to sketch from nature. This ruin is on the spot where there existed a temple in the time of Tacitus, who describes it as the *Ara Ubiorum*. In the old chronicles, a strange king with his army is said to have encamped there for a long while. He held intercourse with devils, for whom he built a temple on the mountain, on which he sacrificed men and women to them. The power of the devils kept him and his descendants on the throne for some while, until the Christian priests put an end to their reign.

" Near this place is a spring of hot water famous throughout Germany as the waters of Draisch.

" Bonn is now visible in the distance, on the very edge of the Rhine. It is quite a pretty town to judge from the houses that lie along the river. All the authorities came out in boats to meet us ; one was filled with young people holding garlands who presented me with flowers. The inhabitants wished me very much to remain for a day with them, but I could not comply.

" Being weary of the beauties of the Rhine, I am quite resolved not to delay my return to Paris by a single day.

" The route as far as Cologne is positively hideous ; on both sides villages situated on a plain without a view anywhere. Having contemplated this landscape for a few moments I went below and remained there for the rest of the voyage, except for a moment on deck to take the air.

" Life on this yacht was very pleasant, notwithstanding we lived together in one room, every one did as he liked, which put me quite at my ease. I did not speak a word for over three leagues as I detest conversation. However, the Emperor tells me I shall be different at the age of forty ; so much the better, that proves I shall have acquired a little amiability which is sadly lacking in me at present !

" We reached Cologne at nine in the evening, greatly fatigued and all suffering from severe headaches, owing to the noise of the cannon which followed us the entire route.

" Hardly had we disembarked before we were placed in a carriage, at least a century old, which was so hard we must have expired at the end of a league, consequently the town of Cologne appeared to us interminable. It is true it is very badly built, there are only 90,000 inhabitants, but the town is so arranged one might easily believe there are at least 200,000.

" I was lodged in the same house as two years ago which belonged to a German Baron who has just died. The rooms are very dirty and full of bugs, but it has a pretty garden with a small greenhouse containing beautiful flowers.

" Cologne has beautiful churches. I recollect visiting a couple of them two years ago. The Cathedral is handsome, and has some very ancient pictures which date from the commencement of painting, also the Chapel of the Three Magi in which their bones are preserved, kept in a golden coffin of extraordinary richness adorned with a quantity of precious stones.

" I was struck by the fact that the relics have been surrounded by engraved stones representing subjects taken from mythology. Over the coffin are their three crowns inlaid with diamonds and coloured stones.

" The Church of St. Ursula is also very beautiful, one of its chapels contains the heads of St. Ursula and her husband, also of her 11,000 virgins. Each head has its separate niche and is adorned with jewels, those of St. Ursula and her husband and one other are kept in bags of taffetas. On one of them hair can still be seen with clotted blood round an enormous wound. St. Ursula's head-dress is still preserved here along with many other precious things in the treasury. In the Chapter of the Canonesses of St. Marie, Marie de Médicis spent the last years of her life.

" Before the Revolution there were 83 churches and convents in this city and over 12,000 beggars. There is also a very pretty botanical garden with a school of natural history. When a Sovereign passes there the guilds parade in front of his windows in the most extraordinary garments. They spared me this infliction.

" In the Church of St. Ursula some very curious paintings may be seen, done in fresco and oil, representing the history of the Saint and her virgins.

" On the 5th we took our breakfast at Cologne, after which I received the authorities until noon ; then we entered our carriages, but I felt very impatient because too few relays had been arranged to admit of our travelling at full speed.

" I believe our journeys are a perfect nuisance to the peasants, who are obliged to provide horses to draw the carriages of the suite. Sometimes a quarter of them break down, then fifty francs for each horse is given in compensation.

" The first stage from Cologne to Bergheim is six leagues, through a superb forest, the country generally is very fine, also from Bergheim to Juliers, which is quite a small and rather pretty place. I think the houses in the town of Bergheim are very like those of Holland on the outside, and seem fairly clean. The last stage from Juliers to Aix-la-Chapelle is seven leagues.

" As may be supposed, it is not possible to travel very quickly, but the beauty of the landscape is sufficient compensation ; the wooded hills abound with orchards and the delightful valleys with streams and cottages. The scenery continues to improve as one approaches Aix-la-Chapelle, where there are many pretty gardens, and the town appears quite close, though still two leagues away.

" On our approach the roads became lined with people. At this season numbers of people take the baths at Aix-la-Chapelle, where we arrived at half-past seven. It looks quite pretty and attracts me more than many places, but it is true I have a weakness for this country, and really am most unfortunate, for this is the second time I have been obliged to pass through here without being able to prolong my visit for a few days to enjoy the beauty of the surroundings.

" I am lodging in the house of the Préfet, M. de la

Doucette; he has a wife who is said to be very amiable, also three charming children. All I know of him is his translation of a German novel, which is incredibly wearisome. I should have been all right there if I could have slept, but a pretty little mouse ensconced itself behind my bed and disturbed me terribly.

"I cannot explain why I was in a very sulky humour on my arrival, but when the Duchess came to inquire whether I would like to see the Cathedral before leaving the following day, I refused to consider the suggestion. She told me how wrong I was, nevertheless I insisted; whereupon she told me many home truths, and as I am perhaps no better than I should be, I soon admitted my error and thanked her for all she had said. Such a friend as the Duchess is very rare at Court! Shortly after, a storm such as I had never experienced burst upon us, and my bad mood disappeared; I think it may be attributable to the atmosphere which had reacted on my nerves.

"After dinner I received the authorities and some little girls presented me with flowers. Next day at eight o'clock, I visited the Exhibition of the Products of National Industry, where the very fine sheets, linens, needles, and pins, and much beet sugar, were particularly noticeable, also a certain kind of cotton fabric made there which is nearly as good as the English. Besides these there were some splendid cotton velvets which are as beautiful as those of Lyons, and quite as pleasant to wear. At Spa they make very gay wooden boxes painted with birds, flowers, or landscapes. From there I moved on to the Cathedral which is very beautiful and of great historical interest, for many Emperors have been crowned there; also I was shown the place where Charlemagne was buried.

"After that I saw the chief relics and those of less importance : the former consist of garments of our Saviour and the Virgin, the latter being the skull and bones of Charlemagne, which are encased in vases of gold inlaid with jewels, while the rest are in taffetas. They told me that during a journey which he made some time ago to Aix-la-Chapelle, M. Corvisart saw these relics and discovered that the bone which was shown as the leg-bone of Charlemagne was really from the arm. This has not been corrected. We had some rings blessed, which I hope will bring me luck, as I have been badly in need of it for some time.

"They also showed us ornaments embroidered by the Empresses, and the State chair of Charlemagne, which is of stone. He was buried sitting in this, but it has since been exhumed, and is now used by each Emperor at his coronation to sit in for a short while.

"At ten o'clock we left Aix-la-Chapelle in torrents of rain, by a very bad road as far as Battice, which is six leagues from there. The country is very fine, abounding in wooded hills and beautiful valleys. This is the coal district.

"I was mentioning the affair of the Chevalier Goffin when some one told me it was even less satisfactory than had been stated, but as the accident happened at the mines of Beaujouc, and had been caused by the negligence and carelessness of M. Micoud (the Préfet), he had decided on a bold action which would be talked of a great deal, so that the original cause of it might be forgotten.

" It is very sad to find how often one is disillusioned on hearing the reason of a virtuous action.

" We did not arrive at Liége, which is eight leagues from Battice, until three o'clock. As we were dying of hunger we lunched at the ' Préfecture,' which was disgustingly dirty ; this is quite unpardonable, as the Préfet is a married man, and the first duty of a wife should be cleanliness. I saw the authorities on my way through and left at four o'clock. Liége is a town of 30,000 inhabitants, situated on the Meuse, having a rather gloomy appearance, but a very fine foundry for cannon.

" On leaving the town, one proceeds along the banks of the Meuse which, although of a softer beauty than those of the Rhine, are in no wise inferior to them in the varied character of the landscape. Many pretty country houses and wooded hills are noticeable, besides enormous masses of rock threatening to crush those who pass between them ; there are also some old castles, but they are rare. We passed Chokrier, Huy, and Schergen, but the scenery is most beautiful between Huy and Namur. I should very much have liked to make the same voyage on the Meuse as on the Rhine.

" We reached Namur at nine o'clock, a small and ugly town famous for its cutlery, but the manufactures are said to be no longer as good as they used to be.

" I arrived quite ill, my health now is not good, which makes me realise I shall not be much longer in this world ; this thought saddens me, for I am so happy, and was exceedingly so before this fatal war. But what is the good of talking of that ? It is far better to hide one's sorrow in one's heart, and resign one's self to the will of God.

" During dinner M. de Croix, the Chamberlain, and his wife, one of my ladies-in-waiting, called on me; they live a few leagues from Namur. I stayed at the Préfecture, which is quite comfortable. The Préfet is an old man. Again in the evening, I received the authorities. On the 6th, at eight in the morning, I continued my journey, feeling sad, for it was beginning to weary me; the route onward is as fine as the one yesterday evening.

" Between Rossillon and Dinant is a rock through which the road has been made, just wide enough for a single carriage. I admit my courage failed me a little at this place.

" We arrived at Givet at one o'clock for luncheon. The town consists of Petit Givet and Grand Givet and Charlemont, a fortress built on a height dominating the town. A stone bridge now connects the two Givets, where I remember two years ago we were delayed for sixteen hours, the Bridge of Boats having collapsed owing to the Meuse being in flood. Some English prisoners hurriedly built a flying bridge whereby we crossed, for which the Emperor gave them their liberty.

" We took luncheon at the house in which the Duchess had lived between the ages of three and nine, which recalled to her many pleasant recollections of it ; afterwards, at two o'clock, we departed, passing by a large building in which all the English prisoners were interned, and appeared to be very much crowded together.

" We proceeded to Fumay, a distance of five leagues, where we left the banks of the Meuse, to climb a very steep ascent into a forest. This continued for more

o

than an hour, until on emerging, the whole of the
Ardennes were visible. A short distance from Rocroy,
we passed an insignificant fortress, noted only for its
name, which recalls the famous battle that was fought
on these plains.

" The country is hideous as far as Mézières, where
we were met by the sous-préfet who had come to tell
us it was impossible for us to proceed any further, as
we should risk breaking our necks. This disappoint-
ment threw me into a shocking temper. I remembered that two years ago we had been very ill there,
and moreover, there was the prospect of getting no
dinner, so, despite the fears that might have over-
come some people, I insisted on continuing the
journey. On arriving at the town the sous-préfet
knocked into General Foache, overthrowing him and
his horse ; fortunately he escaped with nothing worse
than a shock, but the accident might have killed him.
Flowers were offered me.

" At ten in the evening, after leaving the town, we
stopped to partake of a very indifferent dinner by the
roadside, particularly so to me, as I am always upset
by cold meat, and detest bread. After this I lay down
in the carriage, but the road was so atrociously rough
and the carriage swayed so badly that I was as much
hurt as if it had upset.

" At last we reached Rethel on the 3rd at three in
the morning, dead with fatigue. Every one, except
myself and the Duchess, went off to have a second
dinner. I betook myself to bed immediately, but
was unable to sleep.

" Next day after breakfast, we attended Mass and
I received the authorities. The Mayor exhausted

himself by repeating to me over and over again in his harangue, the fact that he was a good *Champenois* (inhabitant of Champagne). This was obvious without much talk.

" Two years ago we lunched here, after which the Emperor met a man in the courtyard, who asked for a pension, explaining he had formerly been the Emperor's writing-master. The Emperor recognised him, granted his request, and clapped him on the shoulder, saying, ' Right, my good friend, you made a fine pupil then.'

" Rethel is a poor little town of 3000 to 4000 inhabitants, which I left at midday; the country is hideous. As far as Rheims, one sees nothing but plains and fields, fertile certainly, but there is nothing agreeable for the eye to rest upon. Towards three o'clock we descended into Rheims, a very fine city ; all the houses were hung with the products of the municipal manufactures. I was offered a basket of gingerbread.

" A league away from Rheims is Sillery, the estate of M. Valeures, where I had lunch when I first came to France. The scenery is pretty enough between Jonchery, Fismes, and Braine (Braisne); there is a pretty little stream in a valley, and the landscape becomes more wooded. Near Braisne I recognised the cemetery where the Emperor awaited me as I passed through. I recalled the terror I felt on seeing him arrive without having been forewarned. It was, however, very good of him to have saved me the embarrassment of the reception which was to take place the next day.

" At ten o'clock we arrived at Soissons where we dined at the Bishop's palace, which is a very fine building, but simply furnished. M. de Beauharnais, I believe, has his rank of Senator here, but it is not yet arranged. During dinner the noise of the pealing bells made horrible music. We entered our carriages again in a fearful storm, to leave Soissons. This is where the King of Holland awaited me with a letter from the Emperor, and was astonished on opening my door to find the Emperor in my carriage!

"The road to Compiègne is quite good. I slept nearly all the way until our arrival on the 9th at one o'clock in the morning. It was quite strange to find myself in such a vast palace, but thankful for a good bed and beautiful rooms—a great comfort. However, this pleasure was not without bitterness, for I thought of the days I had spent there with the Emperor and passed the night in tears.

"Next morning I was surprised to find the changes in the garden which has been laid out in front of the house ; it is very much enlarged and the trees are growing well. My son's room which adjoins my own has been furnished, and is very pretty.

"On the 9th I lunched with my ladies, each of whom related her adventures. We were gay and happy because we were nearing Paris.

"At one o'clock I started in the carriage and arrived without mishap at the Pont Saint Maxence, where an unfortunate postilion who was attached to Prince Aldobrandini's carriage broke his arm. It is really very sad, but I feel thankful my carriage was not to blame, for whenever I am the innocent cause of such a misfortune, I invariably reproach myself with it. Finally, at half-past seven in the evening, we arrived in good health at Saint-Cloud, where I found my son, much improved."

CHAPTER IX

ALTHOUGH after his recent interview with Metternich, the Emperor could no longer doubt the adhesion of Austria to the Coalition, he wished Marie-Louise to be kept in ignorance of it until the last moment. He had promised to assist at the inauguration of the basin at Cherbourg, but being unable to attend himself, desired the Empress to represent him.

He wrote to Cambacérès on August 12: "I wish the Empress to undertake her journey to Cherbourg, but only on her return to learn all this [the affair with Austria]; let her start on the 17th." She intended to leave on the 19th, and wrote: "The Emperor will send me to Cherbourg on the 19th to inspect the New Port." She did not proceed, however, until the 23rd; and the following is her own account of it:

" On 23rd August, at eight in the morning, I left Saint-Cloud for Cherbourg, feeling very depressed and therefore without any interest in the undertaking, for I detest travelling more than ever. Moreover, I am certain my countenance must depress every one, for I feel so sad and have no wish to hide it; also the separation from my son, who is my consolation during the Emperor's absence, is very trying to me.

All this put me in such a bad humour that I was silent during the whole of the first stage, and entirely oblivious to the beauties of the route as far as St. Germain; however, the cheers of the young people from the Ecole, who had come out on horseback to meet me, at length aroused me from my thoughts.

" We changed horses very quickly and afterwards went through an exceedingly beautiful part of the forest. The road as far as Melun with its slopes covered with vines and fruit trees attracted me very much, also the charming country houses, one in particular, which lies on the left, along the bank of the Seine, with a large garden on the right hand.

" Melun itself is a detestable little town if all the houses resemble the one where we lunched, it must be renowned for its dirtiness. We were obliged to pass through the kitchen and a horrible dark passage to reach the dining-room, and risked our lives owing to two or three grimalkins which ran through our legs! But these little accidents only add to the amusement of a journey.

" Two leagues from Melun we passed M. de St. Aignan's house which looks quite attractive; his little children were walking in the garden, looking as pretty as loves.

" The road passed through the avenues of the fine park of Rosny, leaving the ancient castle to the right, along the bank of the Seine, until it ascends a steep slope from which a glorious view can be obtained. The country as far as Evreux is not unpleasing, particularly the approach to the town where wooded hills give a fine effect.

" We arrived at Evreux at five o'clock. The

postilions drove like mad into the town, thereby causing a Brigadier-General to find himself in danger of his life between the carriage and the houses, which gave us a terrible fright. There are truly many things to make one's blood curdle during a journey, and the doctors who always scold when one returns ill after a journey, should really forbid the Generals getting caught between the wheels, and the postilions falling off their horses.

"I lodged at the Préfecture at the house of M. de Micomes (Miramon), Chamberlain to the Emperor, where I was made exceedingly comfortable in four rooms with a very pretty garden in front of my window.

"Some excellent cream was brought me of which I longed to partake, but thought of M. Corvisart and sacrificed myself to his wishes. This was not easy but was commendable, for he never knew of it.

"Evreux is a town of 16,000 inhabitants, with scarcely any commerce. After dinner I received the authorities, who treated me to some rather ludicrous speeches. Little girls came to offer me flowers, and a concert was given in the salon. Verses were sung and a pretty young lady played the harp, also one of the Guard of Honour the bassoon. The garden and the town was illuminated.

"At eight o'clock next day I left for Caen, passing on the left the Château de Navarre, which has a somewhat Gothic appearance, at the end of a fine avenue. We followed this beautiful road across a great plain to the river Thibouville, running through a fairly broad valley surrounded by high hills. A very clear little stream runs at the bottom of it.

I stopped for lunch at a place called La Rivière Thibouville where is a castle belonging to the Chevalier de Reveillac, very badly kept but in superb surroundings. From the terrace a view of the whole valley can be obtained; the village is on the left and on a hill are the ruins of an ancient abbey. On leaving this we crossed a large part of the park where there are magnificent forest trees.

" The country is extremely beautiful, and is quite enchanting from the hill of Lisieux which is rather steep. The town lies in the valley, approached through gardens and meadows and orchards; the scenery recalls Brussels on the side towards Laeken.

" On passing through Lisieux, I was welcomed in a truly touching manner. Generally, throughout Normandy every one is sincerely attached to the Emperor, and the enthusiasm of these good people impressed me much.

" The Mayor and a number of young ladies dressed in white awaited me at a triumphal arch, where twelve charming little fountains had been arranged, from which water was playing. They wished to present me with flowers, so I called out to the Equerry to stop, but General Caffarelli, who feared they were going to eat me (always being suspicious), made a sign to go on, consequently I was not listened to, for in this world those who make themselves feared are always obeyed; the inhabitants therefore were much disappointed. I told them I would take luncheon there on my return.

" The country is delightful to within a few leagues of Caen, with its orchards and meadows, where the finest cattle are fattened; there are some splendid herds and excellent butter and good cream are made in Normandy. I must confess my virture was not equal to the last occasion, for I succumbed to the temptation, regardless of the result.

"The *Cauchoises* (women of the Pays de Caux) are first seen in this part, recognisable at once by their caps, which are pointed and have two lappets. They are a very fine race. We noticed many beautiful peasant women.

"Farther on the landscape is less attractive, for it is much flatter, consequently Caen may be seen from a long distance. We arrived at five o'clock. I was comfortable in the house of a pay-master; the Préfecture was being built.

"Caen is rather picturesque and has a population of between 20,000 and 30,000, who make a kind of lace, also cotton stockings, but they are worthless because they are bleached in lime water. There is a magnificent church built of white marble by William the Conqueror, in which he is buried; it has splendid stained glass windows.

"After dinner I undertook my habitual task of receiving the local authorities. Rank is truly a mixed blessing, for it necessitates the holding of receptions though one may be fatigued, and though longing to weep, the obligation to laugh; and one is never even pitied.

"After this a delightful *fête* was given for me in the garden of M. Michin, at which all the ladies of Caen, dressed as *Cauchoises*, were arranged in a circle. Madame Michin sang some verses in honour of me, accompanied by the choir. After this, one of the Guard of Honour in peasant dress offered

me a bull, meanwhile making a speech delivered with
much enthusiasm, and the prettiest little girl imaginable
was brought seated between two barrels, one of
cider and the other of milk, of which she scattered
some drops. Another member of the Guard of Honour
presented me with a superb bay horse, with the request
that I would name him Calvados. The *fête* ended
with a Norman *Ronde* (roundelay) composed of some
very pretty couplets, and was most charming and
well carried out.

" I left Caen at eight o'clock on the morning of the
25th, thankful to be on the move again, for this
was the only means of escaping the tiresome congratulations of an immense number of persons who
were either hostile to me or at the best quite indifferent.

" The scenery is much the same as that through
which I passed on the previous evening. At ten
o'clock I reached Bayeux, a pretty little town with
7000 people, where a kind of lace is made, similar
to that of Caen.

" Hardly had I put the first morsel in my mouth
when M. de Bearn bothered me to know if I would
hear Mass, asking what I would like to do; his
importunity threw me into a passion. Truly he
deserved the nickname of M. l'Embarras, for it
describes his whole character. Since it was necessary
to make up my mind, I decided to go in procession
to the canopy prepared in this beautiful church,
which is large and Gothic in style ; it also was built
in the time of William the Conqueror.

" After Mass, the Bishop kept me waiting a good
quarter of an hour while he was making his toilet;
usually I laugh at these disturbances, but this time

I was too angry, I was suffering, I was catching cold, and am sure the inhabitants of Bayeux, on seeing me pass, must have said 'What an ugly and ill-tempered Empress!'

"Eight leagues from here we crossed the Day at low tide. This is an arm of the sea over which there is a bridge (as also over the river Conce) and reached Courlan (Carentan), a small ugly town and unwholesome on account of the marshes which surround it. The Emperor has already done a great deal to make the district more healthy, but there still remains much to be done.

"The scenery is everywhere very pretty as far as Valogne(s), a small town famous for its horse fairs, the most celebrated in Normandy.

"The dust was terrible all along the road, which became very bad and stony, and we were so jolted it was impossible to sit upright. The landscape was no compensation, for there was nothing to see but heaths and thickets, while we continued up and down hill, impatiently awaiting the moment when the sea should appear in view. Owing to the tardiness of the Bishop of Bayeux we did not reach Cherbourg until nine o'clock, tired to death, and very anxious to find a comfortable bed.

"I was pleased to find myself once again in the house I had occupied two years ago, for the memories of that journey when I was so happy and light-hearted were very pleasant, but what a difference now!

"My room is the Emperor's bedroom, looking on to a wretched little courtyard where nothing can be seen, and into which all the nasty smells come from the kitchen.

" Cherbourg contains only 7000 or 8000 people, but the town appears much larger than it really is ; there are quantities of dirty little streets and not one fine mansion.

" On the 26th I went to see the dock, which was still empty in spite of all the efforts that had been made ; the water had penetrated a little and had risen over 2 feet, but a dry place had been kept at which I went down. The medals and screwplate had been buried there. I remained there for some moments and was the last person to set foot on it. Caffarelli left one of his spurs behind, which caused us much amusement.

" This dock is a very fine piece of work, it is 50 feet high, and in order to excavate it an enormous rock had to be blasted and hollowed out, they have been working at it for ten years and the dam alone cost two millions : it has an immense framework which is blocked up with earth and clay, a portion of which is to be cut out to-morrow. In order to do this workmen are let down by a rope on the side towards the sea and then saw through it, two steam pumps meanwhile suck out the water that leaks in.

" A second dock is to be constructed which will take two years to complete ; it will not be so difficult because the water will enter from the first basin by a simple dam. It is a masterpiece worthy of the creative genius of the Emperor.

" From there I went to see the place for repairing the large ships, which is entirely built of stone, and a spring of fresh water has been led to it. The whole dockyard is like this, made of enormous stones weighted with lead, constructed by Spanish prisoners.

" One meets convicts here, the murderers wearing green caps, the others red, and it is very sad to see a deserter attached to the same chain as a malefactor. In the galleys here is a Sous-préfet, a Curé with his Vicaire,and a Mayor, the latter for having exempted his only son from conscription. When they attempt to escape the guns are fired three times, and as soon as they hear them the guards station themselves on the roads to St. Lo and Nay, so that all means of escape is cut off.

"Afterwards I received the authorities, two of whom made me such ridiculous speeches that every one burst out laughing. I refrained, but no merit is due to me, for I have not been able to laugh since last year.

"I drove in a barouche towards Valogne(s) to a pretty country seat belonging to M. Dumancel, the park of which is large, but the house atrocious. They do not obtain the advantages they might from it.

"On the return journey, the view is magnificent; from the main road the sea can be seen, with the boats in the roadstead and the ships of the line. We saw two of the enemy's vessels from a long way off, also the camp of the national guard which was pitched on a hill. It is a pity that the road, being so bad, should make the drive such a penance. In the evening some young ladies presented me with flowers. On the estate of M. Dumancel there are some magnificent larches and some fairly large thujas.

"On the 27th, the day fixed for the opening of the dock, the weather was shocking; the sea was very rough, so it was decided the ceremony could not take place before four o'clock in the afternoon.

"I drove to the shore near Fort Kerkervitz (Querqueville) and took a walk. The road was not very good and one sank halfway up one's legs in the sand. I looked for shells but did not find any that were very pretty. We saw a number of little crabs of different colours. Five enemy vessels were in sight, but they could not come near on account of the wind, which was terrific. There is not much good fish to be had in these parts, for what fish there is has to be brought from a distance of ten or twelve leagues, but the crayfish and lobsters are excellent. As there is no fear of being scolded for eating them during my sojourn here, I do so to the point of indigestion; however, I shall be obliged to confess it in Paris, but I hardly think I shall dare to do so.

"I returned at three o'clock. On the journey back we were told that at a place under the sea an ancient forest could be seen at very low water, but though the tide was very low I could see nothing.

"On returning to the Mairie, the Minister told me that the dock could not be ready before half-past three. We were put off like this from hour to hour until six o'clock. I know nothing more vexatious than this uncertainty, for it prevents me doing anything to pass the time, not daring to undertake anything serious, so we consoled ourselves by reading about a dispute between a doctor and a painter, which was very amusing, particularly the doctor's remarks.

"At last, at six o'clock, the Minister came for me

and took us down a slope at the side of the dam, where it was so cold that two shawls and a fur-lined *redingote* were not sufficient to keep me warm.

"The water was already coming in at two openings, and made a cascade 15 feet high, a third aperture was soon forced, but the dam did not look as though it would break. M. Cachin was in a very bad temper because his *coup de théâtre* had not come off.

"During this time all the ships, dressed with flags, were passing in front of the dock. The Admiral caused them to make some splendid and very daring manœuvres by turning completely round. Had he been a little less adroit the vessels must have collided, and undoubtedly one would have sunk.

"At half-past seven, the water had not yet risen, and I was in such a bad humour at having to wait for nothing that I returned home. At nine o'clock the Minister arrived in great consternation to tell us the dam had given way without our having seen it. ' The cascade is still superb : will you just come and look at it ? ' So we hurried back to the dock, but at a quarter-past nine there were no more cascades ; the basin was full, and the water as calm as if it had been there for many centuries !

"They told me that at nine o'clock the increased pressure of the water against the dam had carried away a piece over 30 feet in width, with a horrible crash which had made the ground shake.

"I shall never forgive myself for having missed this spectacle, the more so as it was for this that I had come to Cherbourg. They are now going to remove the rest of the dam.

"The night was fine and warm, which was really

surprising after the cold of the day. We were obliged to enter our carriages again to watch the 10,000 rockets which were to be sent up from the Fort of Le Roule; but, as one misfortune never comes without another, the Prince Albodrandini made us wander through the whole town with the result that we arrived half an hour too late. Perhaps it was no great misfortune.

"Malicious tongues say that the 10,000 rockets were limited to five or six and even these did not go off.

"On the 28th, as the sea was a little less rough, I took the opportunity to make an excursion on the water, so we went out by the Pont des Marchands: in the roadstead we pitched and rolled, but in spite of my wish to be seasick in order to cure my cold, my wishes were not granted. However, the sea was sufficiently rough for Mlle. Montalivet to almost die of sickness.

"We landed on the dyke, which is a league away in the roadstead. For thirty years they have been working on it, but it is not yet finished, and only by sinking stones at random into the sea have they been able to raise up what remains of it. They have now constructed the Napoleon Battery, which has been raised 25 feet higher in the last two years at the cost of incredible labour.

"The Minister had put up a very pretty tent for us, from which we admired the seashore, the town of Cherbourg, the ships in the roadstead, and the sea which had become perfectly calm.

"They showed me the place where, in 1809, 147 men perished in the dyke; they went to sleep one day never to wake up again, the sea having carried them away with the fort. Only one remained who, being drunk, had found shelter in a hole, and was greatly astonished next day to find himself alone upon the dyke.

"There is now a shelter to which the garrison can be withdrawn at the slightest risk.

"On returning to Cherbourg we went on board the ship *Amiral le Courageux*, of 82 guns. We partook of refreshment in the captain's cabin. The Admiral assured us we should find every convenience of life in such a vessel. A battleship, however, is a sorry dwelling. The troops went through some manœuvres.

"I descended to the first and second gun-decks, but did not venture into the hold where the wounded are put, because to do so entailed climbing down a ladder at the risk of showing my legs!

"The other vessels in the harbour are the *Polonais*, *Talemine*, and the *Iphigénie*, frigates, brigs, and corvettes. On our way back to Cherbourg all the vessels saluted us. I find the noise of the cannon very trying, especially so just now.

"In the evening there was a theatrical performance, in an ugly hall which was badly lighted, and only holds 400 people. They gave us *Le Petit Matelôt*, into which they had introduced some verses for me which drew particular attention to my presence. This annoyed me very much and caused me so much embarrassment that I did not know how to hide myself.

"I cannot endure these barefaced flatteries, especially when they are not true, and particularly

P

when they say how beautiful I am! I only like one
form of praise, that is when the Emperor or my
friends say to me, ' I am pleased with you,' which
makes me anxious to do still better; but this evening
I was so angry I coughed for over an hour and could
willingly have beaten every one.

"Again, on the 29th we went on the sea; it was
rougher than yesterday, the pitching was intolerable,
and we were quite unable to get near Fort Impérial
which was the object of our trip ; it is situated on
the Isle Pélée in a line with the dyke. After trying
for two hours we were obliged to return to the place
where the fishing was to begin, and in order to land,
had to get into a small boat while the ship rocked
so much, that we ran a risk jumping from it,
or falling into the sea between the ship and the boat.

"The tide was too low for us to land outright,
so we were carried in chairs to the spot where the
fishing began. I watched it from my carriage ; five
nets were used along the shore as far as the port
of Cherbourg. The casts were not very successful
as only small fish were taken. These included grey
mullet, plaice which are a beautiful green colour,
skate, also quite small cuttlefish which make the
water black when they are touched, also crabs and
an octopus so frightful that I shall not forget its
appearance for a long time. It had a red body
with a pouch and a dozen legs or arms, the colour
of raw meat, which it extended at will and twisted
round one so that it became impossible to release
one's self. The English came so near that we thought
it prudent to retire.

" In the evening all the battleships were illuminated;

they gave a *fête* for me at night which was not bad for this little town.

"I am always amused at *fêtes* given for me personally, because some people dance so absurdly. Among others there was a lady who lifted her foot so high that we could see her leg as far as the knee, also a gentleman who danced like a lobster opening its claws.

"On the 30th there was so much wind we could not go on the sea; the ladies tried it for a short time but were obliged to return at the end of a quarter of an hour. I had a great desire to go too, because they told me it was impossible, being blessed with the spirit of contradiction to a considerable extent; but the Minister would not allow it as he feared the danger. I was therefore obliged to content myself with going over the *Zélandois*, a vessel on the stocks which is to be launched on September 10; it also has 82 guns and is quite finished with the exception of the masts, but is not yet equipped. The place where the *Zélandois* lies is remarkable because it is where the first houses of Cherbourg were founded.

"One reads in the ancient chronicles that towards the middle of the twelfth century, Mathilde, granddaughter of William the Conqueror, Queen of England, and Duchess of Normandy, was caught in a violent storm not far from the port of Cherbourg, and believing herself about to perish, she made a vow to sing a hymn in honour of the Blessed Virgin and to found an Abbey in her name at the place where the vessel could make a landing. The pilot on seeing land and apprehending a safe arrival, cried out in a transport of joy : ' *Cante Regne, vechi terra* ' (Sing, O Queen, behold the land) ! The grateful Mathilde fell on her knees, sang the hymn, and caused a chapel to be constructed near the stream where she landed, which still bears the name of ' Chantereine.'

" This chapel, the ruins of which could be seen down to 1790, was situated a little above the place where the *Zélandois* is being constructed at this moment.

" Constant to her vow, Mathilde also founded the Abbey of Cherbourg, which is served by regular Canons of the Order of St. Augustine, and was razed to the ground by Charles II., King of Navarre, for fear the English should come there ; the chapel of Nôtre Dame du Voeu subsequently suffered the same fate.

" Both the Abbey and Chapel were rebuilt, but a little above the original site. It still stands quite near the Chantereine stream, and the ancient Abbey of Cherbourg has been converted into a naval hospital since the Revolution. The Abbot, now Cardinal de Bayonne, was the last Commendatory Abbot of the Abbey of Cherbourg. Up to the Revolution, Mass was said almost daily in the chapel of Notre Dame du Voeu.

" It is to her, following the example of Mathilde, that sailors in peril from storms address themselves. Scarcely had they landed when they went in a procession to discharge their vows, with every sign of respect and gratitude to the Star of the Sea. In 1790, this chapel was transformed into a powder magazine.

" It is to Charles VI. that France is indebted for the possession of Cherbourg, but the English, profiting

by the unfortunate illness of this monarch, descended
upon Normandy with 50,000 men. Being unsuccess-
ful in taking Cherbourg, which was vigorously defended
by the inhabitants, they bribed the governor with
money, and this place was surrendered to them in
1418. Charles VII., however, drove them out in 1450.

"The inhabitants of Cherbourg remained devoted
to their legitimate sovereigns and made a vow to
God (during the thirty-two years that they lived under
the dominion of the English, from 1418 to 1450)
that if they were delivered from the yoke of these
islanders they would erect in the church, to the
honour of the Virgin, a monument representing
her Assumption into Heaven. This monument was
executed under the direction of Jean Amber, an
architect of Cherbourg, and was completed in 1468,
when it was placed under the vault of the nave of
Notre Dame de la Montée, and is now in the parish
church.

"This model consisted of figures moved by springs,
and represented the coronation of the Mother of
God in Heaven.

"This pious spectacle attracted a great crowd
of people to Cherbourg, during the solemn religious
ceremonies, especially on the Feast of the Assumption.
It gave birth to an illustrious and numerous Con-
fraternity composed of all the nobility of France,
England, and Holland, and was distinguished by having
at its head Cardinal George of Austria, Archbishop of
Valence, uncle of Charles V.

"This monument ceased to work in 1704, on account
of a fatal accident that occurred during the ceremony,
but remained under the vaulting of Notre Dame

de la Montée until the commencement of the Revolution.

"On April 28, 1532, King Francis I. came to Cherbourg. The keys of the town were presented to him by Jean Lasne, Governor of the place, who, at the head of the twelve most notable burghers, delivered an address to his Majesty at the door of Notre Dame.

"The King then took his place under the canopy, entered the town, and was conducted to the church, in the centre of which he placed himself on the throne ; the *Te Deum* was intoned by the Cardinal of Lorraine, who had accompanied the Dauphin on this journey. After this homage, rendered to the Supreme Being, the King retired to the castle, remained there three days, and granted complete freedom to the town.

"The inhabitants of Cherbourg had amassed the sum of twenty-eight thousand francs to complete the west door of the aforesaid church, but Francis, having been taken prisoner at the battle of Pavia, the town of Cherbourg allocated this sum for the ransom of its sovereign.

"In 1366, when the town of Cherbourg belonged to Charles II., King of Navarre, this prince, in order to confer honour on the inhabitants of the city in consideration of the bravery with which they had attacked and repulsed the English in their district, created them all Barons. An inhabitant of Cherbourg was addressed as *père à baron*.

"This town, where affection for the sovereign is a distinctive and hereditary quality, has for its motto these words : '*Semper sui conservatrix*.'

"After seeing the *Zélandois* I embarked on the

basin in order to say I had been all over it. The water was very calm, some vessels were trying to enter by the opening in the dam, but it was not yet large enough, and the sea was so rough they were unable to come through it.

"I went round three times, and afterwards drove to the garden of M. Cachin, the chief engineer, which is situated at the far end of the town, on the road to Valogne(s); it is very small, not exceeding two and a half *arpens* (*arpent* = French acre, nearly four English acres), but is so well laid out that to walk there for more than an hour, always by a different path, is quite possible. The house is quite small, having only three rooms. Farther on there is a billiard-room cut out of the rock, and the garden is arranged to make Le Roule appear to be included in it. It is bounded by a stream of very clear water, up which salmon of twenty to thirty pounds sometimes come in bad weather.

"A very beautiful view can be seen from the top of the garden, embracing on one side the harbour, on the other Le Roule, and behind are the main road and the valleys of Valogne(s).

"The garden was well worth the difficulty of laying out, for when M. Cachin bought it there was nothing but a barren rock, whereas now it is remarkable for its luxuriant growth and beautiful turf. Myrtles and hydrangeas flourish in the open air; plants that require a hothouse in Paris grow here in an ordinary conservatory. The temperature in winter never drops below two degrees and snow scarcely ever falls, but the weather is very uncertain.

"At four o'clock I went home; the weather had

become piercingly cold, which was not good for my cold and made me think I was neglecting M. Corvisart's sermons rather too much, but I wish to live up to my reputation of being a bad patient.

" This evening there was a theatrical performance, happily not a topical piece, in which case I had resolved to have a headache.

" On the 31st, I wished to bid farewell to the sea, which was calm enough when I embarked, but at the end of five minutes such a wind arose, I was unable to do any of the things I had intended. We drifted about at the mercy of the waves for an hour, and I disembarked at the Pont des Marchands to ascend Le Roule by carriage. The road thither is extremely bad and uneven, and it is necessary to make a *détour* to get up it, but once at the summit one is rewarded by the beautiful view seen from this fort, which is not a very important one. Cherbourg lies at one's feet and the hills to the left; to the right is an exquisite valley studded with country houses and woods, and in front lies the sea more than fifteen leagues in extent, which makes the ships look like little black dots. On turning round to look at the view behind me, a gust of wind blew such a cloud of dust into my eyes that I was obliged to give it up and be satisfied to be told that it was magnificent.

" I descended on foot by a dreadful path covered with pebbles and large rolling stones which were dangerous, for if one looked at the view instead of the road one ran a great risk of laming one's self. Two of the gentlemen fell down, which made us laugh very much.

" With maimed feet we arrived at the house, where

I was most agreeably surprised to hear the good
news of the great battle of Dresden which made
our last evening at Cherbourg very lively. Every
one was so pleased, but my joy was not entirely
unmixed, for although we had won a battle, that
would not bring back the Emperor to me; this
thought poisoned all my happiness.

"The next day we departed at eight in the morning
for Caen. The Prince (Aldobrandini) had got it
into his head that the Day must not be passed before
five o'clock, hence we were obliged to go so slowly
that I was seized with impatience; when that
passed it was succeeded by ennui, as in order to
distract myself I went on eating the whole day;
this resulted in indigestion, without the Prince
having any idea of all the annoyances he was causing.
I think he would be readily consoled, for it is his
habit to put every one out of patience.

"I reached Bayeux too late to be able to see the
tapestry of Queen Mathilde. We had only time to
change horses, and reached Caen at ten o'clock.
I left again at half-past eight the following day, and
took lunch at Lisieux, in a very fine mansion.

"We left the old road between Marcheneuf and
Brienne; before arriving at this last little town,
we passed through a charming district, after which
the country became arid and the road hilly until
we reached a very beautiful wood. Farther on is
a fairly steep hill from which the view is quite superb.

"The Seine flowed below on the left hand having
country houses and gardens on both sides of it,
with hills beyond, while on the far horizon others
still higher appeared; at the foot of these the spires

of the city of Rouen could be seen. Thus we arrived
at Moulineaux where we changed horses. I could
not see as far as Rouen for it became dark, but
half a league from there we entered a fine illuminated
avenue where the Mayor was awaiting me.

"The road into Rouen was illuminated round
the Pont de Bateaux, and the boulevards were lit
up in a charming fashion by a garland of lanterns
from one line of trees to the other, with a crown on
each tree. This made a delightful effect from a
distance.

"I stayed with the Préfet, M. de Girardin, a pleasant
man with very good manners. I was accommodated
in the apartment of Mme. Girardin, overlooking
a small garden and the boulevards. The only
drawback was the impossibility of sleeping there
owing to the noise in the street, which was terrible
from four in the morning.

"To-day I arose in a bad humour, having no
news of the Emperor. He is erratic. I realise
he forgets me. Ah, it is only we women who love
with constancy! Men are so frivolous, therefore one
should not take it too seriously; unfortunately
I am not reasonable enough for that, but I shall
punish him by not writing to him for a week, then
he will realise how pleasant it is!

"The weather has been glorious all day. At
noon I received the local officials of whom there
were a great number.

"The brother of the Arch-Chancellor is here, he
is a bishop and a fright. Some one suggested to
me he should be put in a glass case and preserved
as a curiosity and called the sea-monster!

"Rouen is a very large town ; it has 80,000 inhabitants and much trade, especially in cotton goods and sweetmeats. The town presented me with a basket of bonbons.

"I went out at midday, and visited the stone bridge the Emperor is having built, which will be very fine. It was commenced two years ago and will be completed in eight. It is a difficult undertaking because the water is 40 feet deep at this spot. I was also shown the plans for building quays and a bourse which is to be erected on the bridge ; more benefits from the Emperor to his people, how then can they do otherwise than cherish and adore him ?

"From there I went to the valley of Deval (Deville), three leagues from Rouen, which is really delightful. It is very narrow and contains many country houses with delightful gardens ; the wooded hills at either side belong to M. Montaut (Montault), Chamberlain to the Emperor, and one of the richest landed proprietors in this district.

"There are also many manufactures. I saw one very fine spinning mill, which employs over 600 workers, and spins four thousand pounds weight of cotton a month. Many highly ingenious and quite new methods are employed, but I am not sufficiently learned to explain them. This is the only house which has never ceased paying. Next to this the Mayor of Deville had a factory for making indian red, which I went to see. They have a secret for making red dyes, as fine as scarlet. On the way back to Rouen I visited a factory where printed calicos are made. I printed a piece of calico myself ; some of these are exceedingly pretty and are in great demand in this district, where 26,000 pieces are made annually. The garden of this factory, though small, is very charming; they have made a pretty summer-house out of a dovecote; the house is furnished with exquisite taste.

"I returned to Rouen by the road I came on. All the townspeople were on the boulevards. I walked for a little while in the garden of the Préfecture, which is tiny; after which, on entering the house again, I received news from the Emperor which filled me with remorse for what I had written this morning! It is true that though we may not be thoughtless, at least we judge very thoughtlessly. I had a large company to dinner, at which I conversed with the Préfet, and listened with pleasure whilst he said kind things about our friends in Paris; when one is absent it is a very great pleasure to talk of people for whom one feels friendship.

"The young ladies brought me a basket filled with the products of the national industry and were presented to me, after which I went to the play. The hall is very pretty and circular. They performed *Le Billet de Loterie;* the music would have been charming had it been better executed. After that they acted a topical piece for me, much prettier and more simple than that at Cherbourg; otherwise I had decided to strike out half the couplets beforehand. Between the two acts a cantata was given composed by an amateur. The fireworks were extremely good I was told, personally I preferred to go to bed rather than watch them!

"I left Rouen to-day at noon; it took us over an hour to pass through the Boulevards which extended over a league, but afterwards we travelled more rapidly. The country is very fine, and the road continues along the bank of the Seine, almost the whole distance, by many beautiful country seats and much woodland, until, between St. Ouen and Notre Dame du Vaudreuil, it crosses over the Pont-de-l'Arche which the Emperor had constructed at a cost of 150,000 francs. The Seine was not navigable at this point, but with the aid of two sluices and a rock built up from the bottom, it can now be negotiated here as easily as anywhere else. The road as far as Rosny is as pretty as the last we travelled on. We dined in a dirty inn at Meulan and arrived at one in the morning at Saint-Cloud, where I immediately made a vow that this journey should be the last."

What more need be said ?

This journey to Cherbourg immediately preceded the disaster of Leipsic, and from that moment the Emperor held his death at the enemy's hands to be the best solution. The defection of the Austrians had changed the whole situation. The army of 1813 was broken up and forced to retreat in haste, although, formidable to the last, it crushed the Bavarians who attempted to obstruct its retreat to Hanau.

Throughout these disasters, Marie-Louise pursued her customary routine and contrived to show a smiling countenance although surrounded by traitors.

Returning on November 9 to Saint-Cloud, the Emperor was unable to remain there, so moved into Paris on the 20th, contrary to the wishes of Marie-Louise, for it was said, " The air of Saint-Cloud suits her better than that of Paris."

The Emperor endeavoured to ascertain if he could rely on any support from the Government by enlarging on national independence to the representatives, but they replied in the jargon of liberalism. Through Marie-Louise he attempted final overtures of peace with the Emperor of Austria. The reply was more than ambiguous : " This will cause some delay to begin with; afterwards, it will s ɔttle itself, please God."

The fabric was crumbling : nothing remained to Napoleon but his people and his sword ; accordingly, he hastened again to throw himself into battle, leaving the Empress as Regent in Paris, with the remark that " She herself has more intelligence than all the councillors."

It was from a note of Napoleon to Marie-Louise, intercepted by Blucher's runners, that the Allies learned of the decisive movement contemplated by the Emperor, and so were able to seize the road to Paris, where traitors awaited them ready to deliver up the capital and France.

Thus we reach the last journey Marie-Louise was to make as sovereign—a proscribed sovereign—the journey to Blois. Some day, perhaps, a diary of it may be discovered in her own hand, a light-hearted account, designed to be entertaining !

In conclusion, what opinion are we to form of this woman who, for four years, was Empress of the French? For the few months during which she bore the title of Regent, she was nominally empowered by the Emperor to direct everything, until the moment came when she ought really to have taken the reins, then he

deprived her of all authority. There is no evidence
that she possessed the extraordinary powers attributed
to her by her husband, and we are forced to assume
that he was deluded by conjugal affection. The record
of the journey to Saint-Quentin is calculated, indeed,
to alter the prevailing opinion of the intelligence of
the Empress, written only three months after her
arrival in France; Marie-Louise thought, observed,
and wrote like an experienced Frenchwoman. Her
criticisms of her sister-in-law, Caroline, plainly show
what opinion she held of her ; she knew what to think
of Metternich and of the Grand Duke of Wurtzburg,
who were both courting the Queen of Naples. She
described the aspect of the country as well as she
judged human nature.

Then all this suddenly ceases. During the following year her letters to the Emperor were those of a
good, loving little girl. A certain Viennese author
has asserted that she was incapable of love. What,
then, accounted for her anxiety, her paroxysms of
depression, her reproaches, if she were not in love ?
Even if we admit that the Empress loved her husband
passionately, this cannot be said to have developed
her intellect, and the general opinion of her may after
all be well founded. It is by no means impossible
that great timidity, extreme shyness, pride, and the
continual flattery of her lady-in-waiting may have set
up an impassable barrier between the Empress and
the ladies of her court, between Marie-Louise and
society, in a word between herself and France. It is
not likely that Madame de Montebello imparted this

air of simplicity to all that Marie-Louise said and wrote. Her father employed his leisure in making sealing-wax of which he was as proud as of his crown; yet, unless we are to believe he had no part in the policy of his Government and that his Ministers were entirely responsible, we are constrained to recognise a continuity in his purpose; for no matter what adviser he summoned, he persistently followed his own line which might bend or twist, but never broke. One might be tempted to regard the Emperor as the puppet of a caste from which he recruited all his servants, and to which his wife, his brothers, his cousins, and all those who surrounded him belonged, and which influenced his ideas and procedure. But, on the day when one of the most famous of the Arch-Dukes, the only one who may be said to have acquired personal glory, ventured to oppose the Emperor's decisions, describing them as felonious, he was swept aside, and vanished.

Left to her own devices (at least as regards the Emperor, whom Madame de Montebello did not at that time venture to attack), Marie-Louise appears to have developed a sensual passion for Napoleon, fostered doubtless by her admiration for his invincibility, his genius, and perhaps his physical robustness and generosity. He gratified all her wishes and desires for herself and hers; he delighted in providing whatever pleased her, or could adorn her person. She had nothing to wish for, and save that he implored her from time to time not to over-tax her digestion, he enforced few commands. Convinced of her quasi-divine extraction, he respected the prestige conferred on her by birth, and felt himself allied to a sacred being. She was fully aware of the authority with which he had invested her and of her position in his eyes, and while she did not lead him, he occasionally consulted her. Yet she knew nothing of her world, and was not interested (in the seclusion the Emperor prescribed for her, and in which it was her own pleasure to live) in anything beside herself, the Duchess, and the Baron.

What of her son ? Was she even conscious of his existence ? When he was still an infant she feared to take him in her arms, and would not attempt to do so. She would not learn to be a mother in her confidential intercourse with Madame de Montebello, for the latter hated the governess, Madame de Montesquiou, and lost no opportunity of doing her an ill-turn. Without asserting that Marie-Louise did not love her son, the allusions made to him in her diary prove that she did not know him.

The only motive by which she was imperiously dominated was her feeling for her father and her brothers and sisters ; nothing conflicted with this when she was uprooted from her environment. Madame de Montebello alone could have counteracted it, but she was indifferent. No other influences counted—red women, white women, black women, all were of negligible importance in the eyes of Marie-Louise. There was, of course, the Emperor, but the reasons for his ascendancy have already been explained, and chief among them were the imperative and

Q

exacting demands of the young wife's temperament. Herein lies the true explanation of the story : it is not flattering to human nature, but it must be remembered that while fortunate Austria gained by marriage what other nations conquered by the sword, her daughters bore the hall-mark of a fatal dowry.

Wretched woman ! Was it not she who at Blois, in the midst of disasters, allowed two Court officials to come into her room when she was in bed and thinking that one of them was gazing at her foot said, "You are looking at my foot. Don't you think it is a pretty one ? "

"*Oh ! femme, femme—carogne de femme, n'est-ce pas, Figaro ?* "

Frédéric Masson

INDEX

239

THE END

PRINTED BY WILLIAM CLOWES AND SONS. LIMITED, LONDON AND BECCLES, ENGLAND.

www.ingramcontent.com/pod-product-compliance
Lightning Source LLC
Chambersburg PA
CBHW050415260626
47156CB00003B/1027